Heading into Intrigue

– KATHLEEN STEELE –

An environmentally friendly book printed and bound in England by
www.printondemand-worldwide.com

FSC
Mixed Sources
Product group from well-managed forests, and other controlled sources
www.fsc.org Cert no. TT-COC-002641
© 1996 Forest Stewardship Council

PEFC
PEFC/16-33-415
PEFC Certified
This product is from sustainably managed forests and controlled sources
www.pefc.org

This book is made entirely of chain-of-custody materials

FastPrint Publishing
www.fast-print.net/store.php

Heading into Intrigue

ISBN 978-178035-334-0

First published 2012 by
FASTPRINT PUBLISHING
Peterborough, England.
Printed by Printondemand-Worldwide

Chapter One

Rachel Burton awoke with a start. She was conscious once again that her body was oozing its sweaty excretions in spite of the chill of the night air that crept insidiously through any aperture that had inadvertently been left ajar. At this time of the year especially with those clear skies and a full moon to grace the heavens, the night time temperatures performed quite a remarkable act by their drop on the thermometer scale when compared with those of the day. Yet even before she had roused herself properly she realised that she had been subjected to that same dream again. Why this should have happened she had no idea for being a woman in pursuit of her career and according to all reports making a success out of this, it seemed to her to be completely uncharacteristic that such a dream should revolve around the same beach where she appeared to be digging her toes into the warmth of some sand dunes. This most certainly was not a place of which she was familiar and yet the colours unfolded vibrantly in front of her eyes and wherever she was then she appeared to be in a state of some relaxation.

Yet still within the dream this feeling of ambience was not destined to last for long before a figure appeared in front of her. The likeness was not of anybody that she knew or could remember, and yet even as the man drew closer a fear seemed to clutch at her heart and that was the very moment that she had roused. What was more, once roused, she realised that as on previous occasions further sleep was now not an option!

Focussing her eyes on the clock that lay on the table close by she could see that the hour had not yet reached two o'clock. Furthermore she knew full well that she needed her rest if she was to put sufficient effort into her workload that day. Therefore realising the commodity of sleep would now seek to evade her she willed herself into a state of somnolence and listened to the tick of the clock as the minutes eventually turned into hours. It must indeed have been closer to the hour of five before those wished for shades of slumber finally passed across her eyes for the next thing that she remembered was when one certain object was exercising its musical morning notation and she knew that the time had come for her to rise so that she could meet the day with all its forthcoming commitments.

"Guess you look tired Rachel----had a late night?" She ignored the remarks of her colleagues as she sought the sanctity of her own office so that she could endeavour to obey her boss' agenda. If to others she appeared tired then she most certainly was not going to admit to it and with this in mind she took her spectacles from out of their case perhaps hoping in turn that they could prove a defence mechanism. In any case the material she had been given to prepare would be expected to be delivered when she received her summons from the inner office. In truth the middle aged man that occupied that room, even with his kindly eyes, could hardly be considered to be the man of her dreams. But then he was her boss and therefore she must answer his summons.

Even so this person was to surprise her for after handing him the brief she had prepared and after this had obviously met with his approval he somewhat reluctantly passed her a letter containing an invitation.

"I wonder if you could possibly attend to this for me Rachel?" He spoke the words almost as if he felt he owed her some form of explanation. "The fact of the matter is that it is the wife's birthday today and if I am not home in time to take her out somewhere of her own choosing then there will be hell to play!" In truth she supposed that Eric Taylor could still apply a certain pleading look in his eyes, despite his position or his years and more especially if the man wanted something. Yet in Rachel's mind she still held the man a debt of gratitude for finding her this position in accountancy after she had passed her economics degree.

Thus finally leaving the office Rachel glanced down at the envelope she was holding. The invitation was from a Mr Callum Rothwell to attend a meeting at a prestigious city hotel that very evening and Rachel shrugged, well she supposed that she had nothing else planned for that time, besides which she owed Eric more than one favour from the past. Therefore Rachel decided that she ought to return past favours even though such a venue did little to enthral her or enrapture her spirits!

Nevertheless as things were to turn out, from the first moment that Rachel arrived at the venue she realised that it had probably been a mistake for already there were prestigious cars and limousines stopping outside of the entrance ready to discharge their occupants. Folk who, it could be said, were attired in evening wear whilst she herself could merely boast her attire of the day. Matters moreover scarcely seemed to improve when a voice suddenly emerged from out of one of those stopping vehicles; a voice moreover that Rachel immediately recognised.

"Why, it's Rachel isn't it? What on earth are you doing here?" Rachel glanced in the speaker's direction and more especially at that red satin evening wear which the girl was wearing and which clung to her figure emphasising the lines of her womanhood, and it was then that she decided that she most definitely must have come to the wrong place.

"I could ask you the same!" She focussed her eyes on the girl she had attended University with to notice the query in the girl's eyes as she viewed Rachel's own attire. "I actually came here on behalf of my boss. He had an invitation from a Mr Callum Rothwell to attend a seminar here but unfortunately he was unable to come himself!"

"A Seminar?" The other girl definitely appeared puzzled. "There is no seminar going on here tonight. The place has been taken over for the National Awards night for a Children's Charity. Actually it is supposed to be rather a prestigious occasion, which of course one is supposed to dress for!" Again the girl glanced at Rachel's attire with a look that almost resembled dismay.

"I was supposed to be meeting someone by the name of Callum Rothwell here!" Rachel it could be said felt desperate to prove her point. Her invitation had definitely directed her to this place and at this time and no mention had been made of any Award Ceremony. In fact she was positive that Eric had mentioned the word seminar!

"Well the person you mention will be here all right but he certainly won't be here to conduct business matters, not at this time anyway. For you see Callum Rothwell just so happens to be our host this evening!" Rachel must have looked aghast at this statement for the other girl felt bound to interject by shaking her head. "I suppose that one has to admit that Callum can appear to be more than a little eccentric sometimes but this time around there must have been some sort of mistake. Look, why don't you save yourself from further embarrassment by just going to the reception desk and showing them your letter. Perhaps they will be able to resolve matters for you?"

There seemed now to be little else she could do under the circumstances. Besides Davina having given her this advice had now chosen to disappear by mounting the marble steps to join others who were now arriving.

And at least she supposed that by calling at the Reception desk this would go some way towards making her appear quite legitimate amongst those more aptly dressed guests.

The man on the desk seemed more than a little puzzled by her presence but nevertheless he at least extended a point of chivalry by contacting Mr Rothwell who was apparently in residence at the hotel. Whether Rachel had expected to see the man appear dressed for his more formal occasion or not she was surprised at the speed in which he answered the phone call, appearing in person in the reception area, not as one might have expected dressed in formal evening gear, but far more casually, almost as if he had not got around to the act of changing.

"Miss Burton? Eric told me to expect you. Shall we go somewhere a little more private?"

She didn't have time to say anything before the man ushered her into a side room away from the main gathering of the evening. Still she was surprised for Eric had led her to understand that the invitation had been sent to him and as she was standing in for him the other had made no reference to the fact.

"You are looking a little puzzled I see Miss Burton?" He glanced at her expression and Rachel was convinced there was an element of a smile gracing his lips. "Don't be for Eric assured me that under the circumstances you were the best person he could recommend for the task in hand!"

“I’m sorry but I am afraid you have caught me at a disadvantage. I understood that I was merely standing in for Mr Taylor at a seminar because he could not attend himself due to a prior commitment!”

“So that is what the old fox told you, is it?” The smile on his face had now blossomed into a wide grin. “Then I take it that you have no idea what all this is about?”

She nodded as he motioned her to a seat whilst at the same time he produced a dossier from out of a briefcase he had retrieved from somewhere. “I understand that as well as working for Eric you also have a very good degree in economics?” She could only nod her head yet again as she wondered how he came by this knowledge, only to conclude that Eric Taylor must have said far more about her to this person than what she had first credited.

“Then of course you must also be aware of the present economic climate in Europe at this time?”

“Only what I read in the papers and hear on the news although I try to keep abreast of such matters!”

“Then no doubt you will find this file to be very interesting!” She looked at him inquiringly as he placed the dossier down on the table and nodded in its direction.

“I have no doubt you will have plenty of time to read and absorb it during your journey!” He handed her an envelope.

“I am sorry Mr Rothwell but you have me at a disadvantage!”

“One often needs something to occupy them whilst crossing the Bay at this time of the year!”

Again she glanced at the envelope. Matters did not appear to be making sense at all.

“Your ticket and details of the ship you will be going on!” Perhaps he believed that if he spelt it out she would be able to understand better. “I’m afraid that due to pressure of work I will be unable to sail with you to the Island in question but I will be able to fly out and meet you there. Oh you need not worry your boss has already sanctioned your absence from work over the period that I shall be requiring you!”

“Am I hearing this right? You are suggesting that I sail out on this cruise ship to one of the Canary Islands merely to read some sort of dossier. Surely I could read the matter at home and then if necessary fly out to the place when you do?” By this time she had toyed with the papers and seen the name of the craft.

“I’m afraid that is not really an option Miss Burton. Perhaps after you have familiarised yourself with the contents of the dossier you will realise something of the opposing factors in this matter. That is why I have arranged for you to travel out there as a tourist in order to avoid suspicion!”

“But what if I refuse?”

“I am afraid that is also not an option for your presence there is necessary if only in the interests of National Security. Furthermore you have been specially selected for this process. I will now have to ask you to excuse me for as you might well be aware my presence is now required elsewhere. Therefore I will look forward to meeting up with you on the Fortunate Isles by which time you should have been able to familiarise yourself with many of the salient points in the dossier and therefore at that point we will be able to discuss the matter further!"

Suddenly she found that he had gone, leaving her with one very thick folder and an envelope containing her cruise memorandum. "Perhaps I should have said that I couldn't go because I had no passport!" The notion did cross her mind and then she dismissed it for after all the thought of paid leave of absence to be spent on a cruise was perhaps something that was not to be sniffed at although in all honesty her curiosity was still not satisfied as to what role Eric Taylor had to play in all of this !

It was the second night at sea when Rachel eventually realised that Callum Rothwell's words about being careful of certain elements on board began to sound certain warning echoes in her brain. But then she supposed that on the first night, especially after travelling down to Southampton from that more Northerly city, and after rising at dawn to catch the coach that miraculously appeared to have her name included amongst its list of passengers, then her brain had not been in a receptive mode for such eventualities.

The journey itself had passed like a dream apart from its early start but then upon arriving at the docks there had been the usual set of formalities and security checks to go through. Thus once she arrived in her cabin she had wanted more than anything else to try to find some sleep. Not however that this luxury could be claimed immediately because first of all she was forced to attend the obligatory lifeboat drill followed by a meal and then the unpacking of her case. Therefore she had found little time to either sleep or even ponder on the strange situation that had brought her here.

Of course Eric had been more than understanding when she had mentioned taking leave in order to complete this chore. Not that he should have been otherwise for after all it was his suggestion that she should undertake this commitment and she had reminded him of that fact in no uncertain manner the morning following her meeting with Callum Rothwell, although in truth she had already begun to wonder just how much Eric had been involved with the arrangements that followed this meeting

"Did you have a nice time with your wife last night? Where did you get to by the way?" Perhaps her tone had sounded a trifle cold when she finally met her boss, which was hardly surprising considering that it had apparently been Eric who had arranged the meeting for her with Callum Rothwell.

"Thank you yes we had a meal first before visiting the theatre!" Perhaps his words did sound a little apologetic but then it had not been an apology that Rachel had been after for what she truly wanted to know was why she had been apparently singled out to complete this mission for Callum Rothwell. Maybe Eric went some way to answering the question that loomed on her lips when he informed her that she had been the best person he knew who could fulfil the role required by the man with her knowledge of economics.

"Well no doubt he expects me to read and assimilate the contents of some dossier he left with me. Why I do not know at the moment but something more immediate appears to be the fact that I have been placed on a cruise ship to sail around to the Islands whilst he himself chooses to fly across!"

"Callum Rothwell is not the easiest person in the world to understand one has to admit but then he is a very necessary factor in the security of our Island state. Sometimes therefore it is better not to ask too many questions but try to oblige the man!"

Rachel stared at the speaker. A perfectly normal female aged in her mid-twenties all she wanted to do was to live a normal life and not get herself mixed up with people like this. It also showed Eric Taylor in a completely new light as well for she had always assumed that the man was a perfectly ordinary man, even if he proved a little dull at times, who was merely concerned with his business.

"I met Callum at University!" That was a surprise to for she had visualised Eric as being somewhat older than the person she had met. "Oh don't look s surprised I actually lectured there for a time before setting up the business. Callum was an outstanding student and when he left he was rapidly head hunted by the Service. What exactly is his line of work there now I do not know, neither come to that does anyone else for such matters are cocooned in secrecy. But if he requires help on any project then he rapidly assimilates where he can get this from!"

Thus Rachel had left England being little the wiser as to the nature of her new task and with merely a dossier to keep her company. In a certain way it was worth reading the documentation just to see if it threw a light on her proposed role out there.

The second night at sea it was the Captain's reception and having gained an invitation to attend Rachel felt it would be rather churlish to refuse. Thus whilst sipping her bubbly and intermingling with the other guests she was suddenly aware of the interest being shown to her by someone she had not yet met. It was only when the man in question approached her that she realised that this was also a person whom she had travelled down to Southampton on the coach with.

"I believe we travelled down to the docks together?" Obviously this man had also recognised her and feeling that it would be rather pointless to ignore the fact she nodded in compliance.

"Guess that it is unusual to see a lady travelling on her own for unlike the male species they normally like to travel with companions. Brett Chaplain!" He held out his hand as a way of introducing himself.

"Rachel Burton!" She supposed that it was only manners to respond. "And I can assure you Mr Chaplain that the female species does not always require a companion to travel with!"

"Then you are taking a holiday by yourself?" There was something about this guy's supercilious manner that served to annoy her.

"Not exactly a holiday Mr Chaplain. I happen to be travelling on business!"

"You make such an intent interesting Miss Burton! Indeed I had always presumed that business personnel used the airlines as their option in order to cover large distances!"

"Perhaps I am not well suited to flying!" Now she sought to change the subject. This one might be young and in a rugged way he could be considered to be attractive but as far as Rachel was concerned he seemed to be just a little too inquisitive for her liking. "Besides there are certain facts that I need to familiarise myself with before we get to the Islands and therefore this appears to be a splendid opportunity for me to do exactly that!" Well she was telling no lies only being a little economical with the truth. "Are you on holiday yourself then Mr Chaplain?" She tried to turn the conversation back onto him.

"Perhaps I am in a manner of speaking. Or maybe I am seeking the opportunity to seek out some female company!"

"Then I am sure that you will be successful in your endeavours Mr Chaplain, for there are a number of unattached females on board!" She made to move away from him attempting to indicate that she had spotted someone she wished to speak to but escape from Brett Chaplain was not quite that straightforward.

"The name is Brett please and for reference sake I actually think that I have now spotted a suitable companion for the journey Rachel!"

"If you are speaking of me then please forget it. I thought that I had already explained that I have a sufficient workload to last me through the voyage!"

"Now you make that sound interesting. What sort of employ are you in then Miss Burton?"

"I am employed by a legal firm!" And that at least ought to put him off pestering her, or so she promised herself. "And what of your own employ then Mr Chaplain?" She hoped that she was swinging the emphasis of the conversation back in his direction.

"Oh me, I suppose one could consider I was a gentleman of leisure. I was actually between jobs when a relative of mine died rather conveniently and as I was the only blood relative I was left quite a princely sum, enough that is to fund my more expensive hobbies and leave the consideration of the job market until a later date!" The stranger had drawn himself up to his full height obviously considering that the prospect of him having sufficient funds would serve to attract even the more reticent of women.

But not this one, Rachel promised herself with a smile as she finally made to move away. What it was about this person that filled her with trepidation she did not know for on the face of it he appeared young, attractive and with a strong personality. She simply had some inner warning about the man and she remembered what Callum had said about being careful on the journey.

In truth Rachel spent a great deal of the night attempting to study European Law in order to satisfy her current employer. Not that she found the subject desperately interesting and she did wonder what on earth European Law had to do with her own subject matter of Economics. But she supposed the man had been adamant that she needed to study the dossier on the journey out to the Fortunate Islands and as she knew that he was the one who was paying the piper then she decided that perhaps after all she should play her part even though at this stage she still had no idea what her part was supposed to be!

Consequently she was on deck early the following morning in an attempt to fill her lungs with fresh air and also in an attempt to wake herself up, and when the time was appropriate she did not really feel like eating in the Restaurant but chose instead the informality of the Palms Café on board, promising herself that once her cabin had been attended to and in view of the rather turbulent weather conditions outside that made the prospect of sitting on deck a little akin to madness, she would return there and perhaps attempt to catch up with some of the shut eye she had missed the previous evening. It wasn't really considered desirable to bring the dossier to the library to read for she just could not afford to leave it lying about just in case she gained the stigma of Callum's wroth!

Nevertheless her idea of partaking in a quiet and solitary early breakfast was soon to be discarded with the appearance of Brett Chaplain, who upon spotting her made a bee line across the café in her direction indicating that he desired to share a table with her. Why this was the case she did not know for the café was by no means small and at this time in the morning when breakfasts were initially served, there were few takers as others generally adopted a more sensible approach and preferred to cling to their beds for a little while longer.

"I trust you slept well Rachel!" It was Brett who opened the conversation as he gazed at the cornflakes she was consuming almost as if these were a completely alien source of nourishment.

"I had a satisfactory night thank you Mr Chaplain but I guess I am surprised to see you here at this time!" Deliberately she attempted to turn the questioning back onto him.

"Oh guess I am an early riser. I did contemplate going to the gym first but now I am glad I decided against it. But you disappeared early last night. I looked for you but you had already left. Don't tell me that the Captain's reception took it out of you?"

"No, I guess I had other matters to attend to!" She deliberately guarded against telling him what such matters consisted of. It was after all none of his business even if the man posed no threat and such feelings were but a figment of her imagination.

"Well you know what they say about all work and no play?" He suddenly produced a list of the organised events of that day gathered from the sheet delivered to their cabins on the previous evening. "Therefore perhaps you should choose now which of these you want to partake in!"

In truth Rachel wanted to respond that she didn't fancy partaking in any but rather had toyed with the idea of her bed for the next few hours at least in order to catch up with some sleep but then she decided against such a course. After all if she mentioned sleep to this man especially at this time of the day he would only question what she had been doing all night. "Sorry but I guess I haven't found time to study the list as yet!"

"Then please allow me the pleasure of choosing for you. Carpet Bowls does not sound too energetic or we could go along to the beginners dance class, or even go and learn how to play bridge in the card room. I've omitted the pool today as I believe it is still a little too inclement for that!" So it appeared that whatever she chose Brett was determined to include himself in the activity. Still she supposed if there were others present at the time it would not give him much opportunity to try to glean what was in her mind.

"You said that you were going to choose if I remember rightly?"

"Very well then: Perhaps we ought to start off by attending the port talk, there are two of our ports of call on the agenda this morning and I suppose it will not do us any harm to get to know something about them!" Having made this decision the man then strode off to help himself to a full English breakfast and Rachel for her part felt that she lacked the energy to argue with him.

Even though she was tired Rachel had still to admit that she had enjoyed the day and by tea time she had even written off her initial suspicions about Brett now having determined that he was nothing more than a playboy gallant who did not need to be taken seriously and therefore was destined to be good company on that voyage. The rest of her workload she deemed she would have to do once the shadows grew longer and she was confined to her cabin for surely she would be able to manage to plough her way through that documentation before they finally reached their destination.

It was the dancer in particular who caught Rachel's eye when she was persuaded to go to see the show that evening in the Neptune Theatre. Tall and slender in his build and possibly of Eastern European origin the man appeared to have an almost rubberised body in some of his acrobatic movements. The other dancers on stage that night were good but this particular individual most definitely excelled in his movements. Yet the reason he possibly caught Rachel's eye in this manner was that she had previously seen the man on deck when after escaping from Brett for a time she had endeavoured to catch some of the current sunshine and marvel at the strength and size of those Atlantic rollers that demanded that they should catch the eye of man to prove that in their own territory they were a force to be reckoned with, for the stranger had almost possessed a haunted look about his eyes.

True the ship had now passed through the worst of the weather once it had negotiated the notorious Bay and yet such great walls of water almost gave warning to some rogue wave that was to follow. Now the waves no longer felt the need to break with its characteristic white froth for they appeared to be ever rising even as the ship continued to plough onwards through them, as if determined to continue its onward journey in order to reach its first port of call on time. At this time also one of the lifeboats stationed just above this level on the boat creaked almost in protest almost indeed as if it was now seeking to break free of its shackles and experience these oceanic currents for itself.

The dancer had obviously been watching her expression as she had eyed the tumult and possibly thought that she needed some form of reassurance for he ventured to extend some kindly support.

"You are perhaps a little worried Madame?" His English was remarkably good and possibly the only factor that gave away the notion that this was not his native tongue was his accent and the pronunciation of some typical British words.

Rachel remembered shaking her head with a smile. "No as a matter of fact I was simply fascinated watching the ocean. My main desire was simply to get some fresh air for there seems to be so much going on inside!"

"That is indeed a truth for the passengers always wish to be entertained and therefore perhaps they forget to give credence to the vagaries of nature!"

"I take it from that you are not a passenger yourself?"

"No I am currently employed by the Show Company that is present on the boat at this time!"

"Then you enjoy travelling?"

"It is a job Madame and jobs are not so easy to come by in my Homeland!"

"Then you are not English?" Rachel bit her lip for it was rather a silly thing to say considering the job market in the U.K. at the present time. Fortunately the man did not appear to take offense.

"No my home is in Croatia, only I have not been home for some time. So do you cruise often then Madame?" It appeared that he now wanted to change the subject.

"No I guess that this is my first time!"

"So you enjoy your holiday?"

"But of course!" There was no point in denying it for she had enjoyed the day even if her true purpose for being here was not on holiday.

"And tonight you will be coming to see the show?"

"I believe so, yes!"

"That is good for tonight I will dance for you Madame!"

She sought to make some reply but by the time the words had formulated themselves in her mouth the man had disappeared almost indeed as if he had been a spectre appearing on that otherwise deserted deck and even now she was appreciating his movements on that stage.

It was at the end of the performance when the players came to take their final bow that Rachel believed that the dancer was trying to seek her out in the crowd. Thinking that this was after all her imagination she would have discarded the notion had not Brett suddenly passed remark that indicated he was musing in a similar manner.

"The male dancer, the tall thin one, he appears to be looking in your direction?" It was a question and yet Brett's tone of voice indicated that he appeared to be non-too pleased with the idea. A thought that to her mind appeared simply ludicrous.

"Actually I met him on deck earlier on this evening after you had left me to get changed!"

"But he isn't even English!" Brett spoke the words almost as if this gave the fellow no right to be speaking to any of the passengers and Rachel frowned for she had never assumed that Brett, despite his bombastic nature, could be racially motivated.

"No, apparently he comes originally from Croatia but with the sort of skills he has I would have thought he could have got work anywhere!"

"Maybe, but he is still not a passenger!"

"Guess I never branded you with the label of being bigoted. Still I suppose I am still on a learning curve as far as yourself!"

For a moment it almost appeared that her words had found a target but then he laughed. By this time the players had all left the stage and they themselves were in the process of leaving the theatre.

"Then please ignore my warbling. Perhaps after all I was merely jealous that someone else had caught your attention in my absence!" Again the man was turning on the charm and yet a strange suspicion was growing in her heart as to whether Brett was everything that he was purporting to be!

Although late for bed that night Rachel was still determined to complete her self-imposed quota of work on the dossier before she went to sleep. Consequently with eyes that now resembled little more than slits in her head she fought off the sleepy state that threatened to overcome her and found herself instead reading about the laws on Immigration. Not that at any other time this would have been of any interest to her and she still could not quite comprehend what this had to do with the Euro and the default payments that currently found press headlines. Quite possibly it was because of her meeting with that dancer earlier in the day that gave her a renewed interest. Not that by any stretch of the imagination did she believe that he had come to Britain in the first place illegally, her interest really lay in what had been his prime motivation for leaving his homeland.

Alas however she found that the tendrils of the night were rapidly creeping up on her so that her eyes quite frankly finally refused to function and she had to lay the file to one side. Still as she settled down for the night she did wonder what Brett would have to say if he had known for one moment what she had been about. There again she had to remind herself that this man, even if for his own reasons he had befriended her, was not exactly her keeper and once they reached the Islands their paths would inevitably part. What her role would be upon their arrival she still did not know and she imagined that Brett would find it very difficult to understand why she had taken on an assignment that she knew nothing about with a person whom she knew even less. The man most definitely would not have approved and the thought of his expression if he had but known lulled her to sleep on a note of merriment!

Whatever her secret thoughts were on the matter, Rachel was nevertheless due for something of a shock the following morning when following breakfast Brett suggested she should go and get her costume.

"What on top of our breakfast?" At least she made her feelings on the matter felt. Granted the pool he was speaking about was both indoors and heated so that it registered a comfortable temperature but this activity was not something that she had anticipated, For starters she actually wondered whether in her mad rush to make it to the coach she had actually packed her costume for it was not something that would openly suggest itself at this time of the year. Fortunately however she suddenly remembered that there had already been one that had been left in the case from a previous holiday, one that she had not removed because so far it had remained unused for in truth the general idea of stripping off to enter some pool did not particularly thrill her.

"By the time you are ready and we have made it up to the top deck then our breakfast will probably have settled if that is what is worrying you!" Brett appeared so determined to complete this task therefore any thought of actually refusing to take part seemed to be rather churlish!

Thus taking the obligatory shower before entering the pool, much against her reasoning for she had already showered once that morning she noticed a girl leaving the area. Yet what proved more interesting was that the girl had obviously been crying and had therefore probably come to this area for a little bit of solitude.

"Look I'm sorry. Perhaps I shouldn't have barged in here disturbing you?"

A pair of tear stained eyes looked back at her and it was then that Rachel recognised yet another person from out of one of the shows, this time a member of one of the show bands.

"You have really nothing to be sorry about!" This time the girl spoke fluent English with no sign of any accent. "After all it is really not my place to be here!"

"You came no doubt because you desired a little peace and quiet and no one can blame you for that. Is it something serious or a matter you cannot speak of?" A feeling of empathy went out to the girl, probably some failed love interest, and Rachel felt thankful for her maturing years. At least she believed that she was well and truly through that stage for the girl in front of her appeared barely out of her teens and at a time in her life when all love interests were serious and nearly everyone finished up sooner or later with a broken heart. She herself had suffered a similar experience whilst still at university. In fact it was probably only having to produce the course work on time that had returned her back to the field of normality.

"My boyfriend is one of the dancers with the Show group only unfortunately the band I am with claim that he makes an unsuitable escort for me and that if I wish to stay as their lead singer then I must forget him!"

"That seems to be a little bit harsh if I may say so!"

"But not totally the whole story, for there is another in the band with me who wishes to claim me for himself and not only that he is supported by our group leader who now claims that Adri is an illegal immigrant anyway!"

A sneaking suspicion surfaced in Rachel's mind that this was the Croatian dancer who the girl had been speaking about and of course as the majority of the band of musicians were of Irish descent then the chances were that they would close ranks on the slightest pretext.

"The only advice I can offer you is to stick to your guns!" Rachel decided that these words were rich coming from her. After all she had been determined to complete this journey on her own and now found she was practically sharing every minute of the voyage with Brett therefore one could hardly say that she had stuck to her own prior decision. Still the girl smiled rather wanly at her before leaving and Rachel decided that she had better get that shower fast less Brett came in the place looking for her.

He was outside of the door waiting for her when she emerged wearing the scowl of someone who thought he had been stood up. "I must say you took your time!"

"I was simply talking. Exchanging words, the art of conversation that men appear to hold in such high regard!"

"So you were holding court with the singer were you? I saw her leave the shower room just before you came out!"

"The same! Tell me is there any rule that says that I cannot do that?"

"And what did you find so interesting to talk about then, fashionable swim wear?"

He had ignored her question and it was there and then that Rachel decided that Brett was just a little too inquisitive about her life and once again warning bells seemed to sound in her head but then as the pool awaited them there appeared to be little she could do about it at that moment in time.

Perhaps it was with this notion still fresh in her mind that when the ship docked in Madeira, Rachel determined to venture ashore on her own. Fortunately for her there was a sightseeing bus that she was able to catch at the quay. A sort of Hop on hop off at will service that toured the salient points of the city and Rachel decided that this would suit her fine. She knew full well that Brett had his own plans for taking her ashore but perhaps because of his damned attitude towards the male dancer she had decided to leave the ship without him and at least spend part of the day in her own company. Folk were getting on and off that bus at every stop but they had travelled almost as far as the cable car which transported those who wished to descend the terrain in a wicker basket to the starting point of this tourist attraction. Not that Rachel had any preconceived notion of partaking in this sport and she shuddered at the thought that had Brett been with her then by this time they would probably have been rising to dizzy heights in the cable car.

As these folk alighted from the bus others appeared eager to clamber on board and one person in particular caught Rachel's attention for the man was speaking on his mobile in syllables that anyone who had a moderate hearing acumen could easily hear. Although the language he spoke was not English Rachel had enough understanding of Portuguese to be able to catch some of this conversation and although she couldn't quite understand to what he was referring the word Europe attracted her senses and she craned her ears to listen for more. This factor had just extended her interest when the man was joined by a woman, her main criteria appearing that she happened to be dressed in emerald green apparel which seemed to be a little ludicrous at this time of the day. Moreover her emerald green outfit was complemented by painted ginger nails. Perhaps this sighting had really little significance but it was just at that moment that the clock on the church tower began to ring out the midday hour and it accompanied this by following it with a certain melody. It was then that the man in question gave the woman a meaningful look almost if this sound bore some hidden significance. Rachel heard no more for their heads were by now immersed in some papers which was now holding their attention!

★ ★ ★ ★

Chapter Two

Rachel had most certainly not been expecting to be contacted during the voyage by Callum Rothwell, but there again in all truth she did not really know what to expect from that man, nor indeed what he for his part, expected of her. Of one thing she was certain however and that was she was totally sick to death about reading up on European law for after all this was neither her subject nor her interest and she was now begrudging the time spent during the night time hours swotting up on a wad of facts and figures that were not of the least interest to her and which, if she had followed her instincts, she would gladly have confined to the rubbish bin!

Besides Brett was now beginning to question why she was always claiming that she needed to retire early for the man was a definite night hawk and he was not particularly pleased when she left him at what he considered to be a quite unreasonable hour.

"Surely you can't still be feeling tired?" He regarded her quite disbelievingly for to his mind it was the older folk who were the ones to seek their beds at this time of the night and not someone of her age.

"Oh I still have some things to sort out in my cabin!" Her excuse was feeble and therefore it exacted little credence from her companion but as far as she was concerned this excuse had to suffice.

The first sign that Callum Rothwell was still very much alive came in a recorded message delivered via the Digital receiver in her cabin. The message simply stated the he intended to contact her by phone at 6pm the same evening, which to her mind was an ungodly hour especially considering that this was the time for the evening meal to commence. That of course was the reason why she had to find some excuse to eat in the Palms café that evening because of its flexible dining times rather than in the main restaurant. To make matters even worse it also happened to be one of the formal nights on board before the ship reached its first port of call and Brett had already been sporting his tuxedo in readiness.

"Then perhaps you could enlighten me what the hell you are about? Why even the entertainers are dressed up tonight. Not only that but I have heard that after the meal there is a very good violinist to entertain us!"

"Look I am sorry but it is just something that I need to attend to!" He was expecting some sort of explanation but there was no way she could confide in this man. "Look I'll tell you what, you go and have your dinner in the Restaurant and then hopefully I will see you later!"

"Sorry but that is not good enough!" He managed to affect a fit of the sulks for her benefit. This of course was an expression that Rachel considered would be perhaps more apt if it had come from a woman: In all truth she had not made up her mind about this character yet. Was he quite as genuine as what he tried to make out or was there still some underlying mystery about the man? "All right then, do what you have to and then we will eat in the café if that is what you want!"

Even so whether Brett appreciated her actions or not she took her leave and as the lifts appeared to be busy at that point in time she decided to take the stairs. She had descended about half way down these when she spotted the girl, who at the time appeared to be in the midst of a flood of tears and the dancer together. Of course neither of them recognised her as she passed by because at the time they appeared to be having something of a heated argument.

"There certainly must be something in the air tonight!" She grimaced as she thought of her own wrangling with Brett. "Maybe we will all be better when the boat docks again for perhaps we have been at sea for far too long!"

Yet Callum's voice when she answered the phone did not appear to be in any way conciliatory towards her. "I do hope that you have spent a great deal of your time studying the dossier that I gave to you for I consider that your time on board ought to provide a splendid opportunity for you to familiarise yourself with the salient points of European law!"

For a moment Rachel did wonder whether the man had some sort of telepathic instinct that automatically highlighted her own discrepancy in this area but nevertheless she still grunted whilst hoping he would take that to be some sort of affirmation to his question.

"Still the true reason for this call is that if you remember I did warn you to be vigilant and it has recently come to my ears that one such suspect just happens to be on board your ship. I do not know whether the person with the name of Brett Chaplain has made himself known to you yet but if you do come into contact with him then please stay clear of the man. The other thing I wish to tell you is that I will be meeting the boat at Santa Cruz when you dock there. I admit that initially I did not think the boat put into port at that place but now something has come up and as a result I have now had to revise my own plans that initially incorporated the Caldera in La Palma. Still as both of these places come within the jurisdiction of the same authority, I presume that the place itself makes little difference. I will be awaiting your arrival in the Terminal buildings on the quayside when you arrive!"

"All of which is just dandy considering he has not bothered to explain what exactly will happen then!" The words of objection scorched her lips but by this time, having imparted his message, he had ended the call thus leaving her in a state of some frustration.

Venturing back along the companionway however it was a scene of some turmoil that met her eyes, not least augmented with members of the ship's crew dashing hither and thither and the area leading to the stairs now cordoned off. Mesmerised with what was currently happening and with her mind still fixed on the telephone call she had just received, Rachel hedged forward only to be stopped by a serious faced member of the crew.

"I am afraid that the stairs are currently out of action Madame. There has been some sort of an accident there!"

Accident? ----- Well she supposed that after three days at sea and with the waters now calm no one had any excuse for falling down the steps at this time. Nevertheless even as she hesitated wondering whether to return to the other staircase she saw the doctor descending down the flight of stairs that was now cordoned off, the man shaking his head. Upon this action one of the ship's officers currently on stand -by reached for his mobile. Rachel heard the word police uttered before the folk now milling around the bottom of those steps, still wondering what was going on, were quickly dispersed and packed into the two remaining lifts to remove them from the scene.

"So what has been going on then? What is all the fuss about?" It was Brett who was waiting to greet her when the lift finally stopped for apparently news that something had happened had by this time filtered through to the Restaurant area.

"I believe that there has been some sort of accident on the stairs. At least we were all filtered off to use the lifts in order to get us away from the scene!"

"It sounds like some accident I must say. I have heard that the police are now being flown in for apparently the girl is dead!"

Rachel knew of course that there was a helipad on the top deck for emergency use but the enormity of what Brett had said was enough to make her blood start to run cold.

"Who was it do we know?"

"From what I have heard it was the girl musician from out of the Show Band. Apparently her neck had been severed in two places. I guess her attacker must have been someone who was pretty strong to have done that! Yet you say that you didn't hear anything, after all she must have shouted out?"

Rachel's thoughts returned to the young couple she had seen earlier. In truth the male dancer was strong for they had already witnessed an example of this on stage. But there again he was supposed to have had feelings towards this girl!

"I'm beginning to think that you know far more about this incident that what you have let on!"

"I passed the pair on the stairs a short time before the incident. I suppose I must admit that they appeared to be having some sort of argument, and the girl was in tears, but what it was all about I have no idea. When I saw them I put it down to some sort of lovers tiff!"

"Then I expect the police when they arrive will also want to question you as you now appear to have been the last person to see the girl alive!" Brett now appeared to be veering into a mood of excitement over the tragic affair and Rachel decided that this was certainly not a healthy sign. Besides she could still remember the warning that Callum had given to her about this man.

"I suggest that for the time being we try and concentrate on going in for our dinner. After all that is what you were stood here waiting for my return so impatiently for isn't it, the reason you chided me for going back to my cabin?"

At least he seemed to agree with that argument and Rachel decided to leave the rest until later!

It was sad to see Adri handcuffed and in the custody of those security guards. Even as she inadvertently passed by the scene however she became conscious that the Croatian was once again looking in her direction this time with an almost pleading expression in his eyes. She would have carried on walking however but someone appeared to have also spotted her on the stairs earlier on when the two were rowing and now one of the stewards called her over to question her about it.

"I can only say that I witnessed them having a perfectly healthy argument when I passed them by!" What else could she say? After all folk simply having a difference of opinion did not often constitute a murder to be forthcoming but nevertheless her name and cabin number were recorded and she was advised that she might be required to give evidence at a later stage.

That later stage came when the body and the man arrested for murder had both been removed from the ship, with the Captain still fuming because such a hold up whilst the police had boarded had put him behind schedule in reaching his next port of call. It came at a time when Brett had also descended the stairs to look for her and was not particularly in a good mood either for he believed that she might be standing him up.

"When you have finished with Miss Burton, I happen to have need of her!" Rachel marvelled at the way that Brett approached the police officer who had come on board in such a gruff manner and for a moment wondered why he assumed he could speak to a policeman in such a way. Nevertheless much to her surprise his words did seem to have some effect for the young officer after turning to voice objection from this intruder opened his eyes wide to take in the stance of the man before shrugging his shoulders and letting her go.

"So what exactly happened then?" Brett still demanded to hear the truth from her own lips as they finally managed to catch the lift back again to a scene of normality.

"You were right in your assumption that the police would want to question me when they arrived on board!" She could already see him preening himself at her words.

"Poor kid!" His sympathies were obviously still with the girl even though she had not currently mentioned her. "Still I always thought that there was something strange about that Croat and no doubt with his strength he had the power to be able to do it!"

"But what if he wasn't the one to blame?"

"Oh come off it Rachel, there was apparently only the two of them there when it happened. You were witness to the fact that you saw them arguing as you passed by. No, the police have got the right man!"

It seemed to be pointless to argue with him any further on the matter and therefore it was easier for her to lapse into a mode of silence. Initially he had been pestering her to go with him to see the volcanoes when they arrived at La Palma but what with first Callum and his dictatorial attitude and now Brett sparring for an argument Rachel decided that she would probably be far better off going ashore on her own. That was the reason why after the meal she sneaked away to reception to see if there were any vacancies left on one of the tours from the ship and fortunately for her, or so she decided, there just happened to be room on the tour to the Caldera de la Taburiente. Thus having collected her ticket Rachel vowed to tell no one for to her mind it would be a relief to get away from the male species at least for a short time!

The walkers had set off on their self-appointed pilgrimage, which was to a particular vantage spot overlooking the Caldera and therefore the place where the coach had parked was now consequently quiet for which Rachel had felt thankful. It was not that she bore any of the party any malice but in truth after the turmoil of Callum turning up in La Palma especially after she had relented against her first intention and had agreed to go out with Brett that day, if only to attempt to allay the suspicion the man now appeared to be having of her, was enough reason to persuade Rachel to follow her first instincts and attempt to find some solitude all on her own!

Yet now, even though she had succeeded there was something about this Canton of Aero where the Caldera was situated and where once King Tanausu ruled in peace until he was tricked and kidnapped by the Spaniards and subsequently starved himself to death during the hazardous journey back to Spain, which made such tranquillity uneasy. Indeed it was almost as if the Roque de los Muchachos held some dark secret and was awaiting its chance to claim vengeance for all those souls that had departed. Perhaps in truth one could say that there was a feeling of being drawn ever closer to the abyss where many brave souls had met their doom and where the undercurrent of sea water was slowly eroding away the mass from beneath ones feet as nature itself slowly executed its promise of the Tsunami that must surely follow and half of the land mass would topple down into the ocean from whence it first came!

Rachel did not know what it was that appeared to be between Callum and Brett yet she most definitely sensed the feeling of hostility and it was this same feeling that she got even now high up on the edge of the Caldera.

A shadow passed her by as she sat trying to switch her mind off matters and concentrate instead on the guide book in her possession. At first she thought that the sun must have disappeared behind one of the clouds that hung over the mountains like a lace table cloth and that the weather had turned dull like it had been on the Eastern side of the Island before they had passed through the tunnel of weather! But the sun still shone round about her and Rachel felt her fear intensify as she glanced up at the figure now paused in front of her. This she gleaned was a stranger but someone dressed in the ancient regalia of the Island and carrying with him a long pole by which he could comfortably traverse the cliff face thus preserving the tradition that remained exclusive to this part of the Archipelago. For a moment she thought that the stranger was about to speak to her but if that was his intention such conversation was halted by the approach of yet another figure who alighted from a taxi positively blazing in anger. Upon the sight of this the native decided it was time for him to disappear over the cliff edge and leave her to face the wrath of Callum Rothwell on her own!

"Don't you ever dare to pull that one on me again! That is at least not whilst you are supposed to be working for me!" His affront left Rachel speechless for she considered that she was not the one who was at fault. "I followed you here by taxi!" She wondered whether he considered this to be some sort of explanation for his presence here.

"Why?" It appeared to be a logical response in her eyes but it was certainly not as far as Callum was concerned.

"Because with your behaviour as well as the people you choose to associate with I wonder whether you are actually trying to put the European project in jeopardy!"

"I am sorry but it appears that I fail to know anything about any such project. Therefore if I do not know then how am I supposed to be putting anything in jeopardy? Perhaps therefore you would like to illuminate further on the matter!"

Her companion growled but was obviously in no mood for such explanations. "Legend has it that the Caldera has ears!"

Now she couldn't make up her mind whether the man was trying to lighten the current mood or not! "It also has a presence here that demands to be felt!" Her instincts told her that she was right to challenge him.

"And no doubt you are in the midst of enjoying this intangible mystery?"

"Yes as a matter of fact I am even though I initially came to seek the peace as well as to get away from a couple of squabbling males who were acting like adolescents!"

"Then I suppose I ought to apologise. I simply saw red when I spotted you with Brett Chaplain especially after our previous conversation. As far as my arrival here on La Palma, well shall we say that it was simply opportune. Besides which there are matters that I need to discuss with you before we arrive in Tenerife!"

"And just how do you propose to do that. How can we possibly have time to discuss anything before the boat sails?" Immediately Rachel had spoken these words she realised that she had proverbially put her foot in it. Naturally there was much that she needed to discuss with Callum Rothwell, starting off no less with the question of what exactly she was supposed to be doing out here.

"Again the answer to your problem is really quite simple for you see I already have a cabin on board! It just wasn't convenient for me to take up the key to it in

England: that was the reason why I said that I was going to fly out. The second matter you mentioned has kindly been solved for us by the purser who has kindly provided a private room where we can engage in private dialogue during the next forty eight hours until we reach Santa Cruz. Changing the subject however I believe you had some excitement on board last night, a murder no less?"

"To which I could easily be recalled as a witness even though I have given my statement already!" Rachel pulled a wry face; no doubt Callum would have something to say about that as well!

"That won't be necessary for I have already cleared up the matter for you!"

"Well thanks a bundle. I am sure that the police welcomed your interference!" These at least were the words that came to mind, but nevertheless she decided to attempt to adopt more concern in her delivery. "In actual fact I felt sorry for the dancer who was arrested. I have the strangest feeling that he was not the person who committed the crime even if he was in the wrong place at the wrong time!"

"He was a Croat wasn't he?" She now wanted to hit out at him for using that tone of voice for to her mind it sounded far too much like the assumptions that Brett had made. "Now I wonder ----!" He stopped and she suddenly noticed an expression of puzzlement on his face but this soon appeared to evaporate. "-------But now for something different! As we appear to have at least buried our initial differences perhaps you will now tell me what you think about the Caldera?"

"Eerie is possibly the word I am searching for!"

"How about using the word captivating instead? Perhaps it is the sort of place that can possibly capture ones imagination and is also capable of throwing illusions into the spectre of life?"

Rachel recollected her own earlier thought on the matter but she was resolved to leave those in the past. What seemed to matter most was that after quite a struggle she had finally succeeded in reaching a level playing field with Callum and she decided that she liked him much better when he was behaving in this manner.

The group who had followed the track to the vantage spot were now beginning to return and she glanced now in Callum's direction wondering at the same time if he would now expect her to go back to the port with him in a taxi. Apparently the man had prejudged her thoughts.

"Tell me were there any spare seats on the coach you came in?"

"Well they apparently saved three for our escort of which there was only one!"

"In that case please consider that you now have two escorts back to the ship!" He smiled almost disarmingly in her direction. "Anyway I guess it will save me the taxi fare if I can cadge a lift. I'll go and have a word with the guide!"

It certainly did not appear to take Callum long to persuade folk around to his way of thinking for the next thing that she knew he was sitting on the seat beside her on the coach, but not without first issuing forth this rejoinder.

"I wonder what our friend Brett Chaplain will have to say about this if he happens to be waiting for you to return when the coach arrives back at the port."

Callum was right in one respect for Brett was stood on the quayside positively fuming when they arrived back at the ship and that was when Callum, whether out of devilment or not, stepped to one side in order for Rachel to handle the torrent of words that were to follow.

In fact Rachel actually believed that the man was laughing as Brett's greeting flayed her. But then Rachel was not one to give in so easily. "I'm sorry if that is the way you are thinking Brett but I am afraid that I felt that I simply needed some space today!" At least now that Callum was out of the way she could make an attempt to regain some self-respect. Upon these words the one she had intended to turn full circle and walk away, but reality was not quite as simple as that for Callum had not moved far.

"Well I guess that is all right for the time being. But I wonder how you will handle the situation when there are two of us plying for your favours at the same time?"

"So you are suggesting that I won't be able to handle such a situation, is that it?"

"Shall we say that I will find it most interesting to watch your efforts?"

This man was positively incorrigible. His previous mode of seriousness had now shifted and he actually appeared to be enjoying the situation. She thought back to seriousness of the man she had briefly met in England and found it nigh on impossible to believe that these two characters were the same person and she wondered how on earth she was going to be able to work with him.

The answer to her problem was that in fact she found that it was surprisingly easy to work with Callum after all. After the skirmish when they had returned back to the ship Rachel had decided that it was probably best for her to avoid both of them at the evening meal and afterwards she took to the deck to fill her lungs with fresh air before retiring fully determined that there would be no night life for her that evening. Not that this stopped her from hearing the disgruntled tones of some of the other passengers because following on from the tragedy it appeared that the cast of two of the shows on board had been depleted and the other members were now in the process of trying to adapt their acts. This had placed the onus for the entertainment on two of the remaining acts which were only guest artists employed for the duration of one cruise. Not that this business entered her head whilst she strode the deck although upon reflection she hoped that this argument would persuade the other two that this was the reason for her absence that night.

The next morning Callum, who met her as they had arranged, made no mention whatsoever of her absence the previous night for today Callum was very much in the mode of the business executive. His first question was to demand exactly how much she had managed to read and digest of the dossier he had given to her.

"I don't think my response will either delight you or meet up to your expectations!" She decided that perhaps it was better to get this off her chest for a start especially after she remembered those boring nights when the reading of them had sent her to sleep. Well someone once said that confession was good for the soul.

"In truth maybe I was expecting too much!" She began to wonder what had made the man's tone suddenly soften for in the past he had been determined that she had to read the blasted thing from cover to cover, not to mention understanding what she was reading about as well! "The real importance is that you should have at least some knowledge of European Law for after all we don't want to find ourselves treading on anyone's corns, do we? This------!" He handed her a foolscap sheet. "Is where your economic skill comes into use?"

The facts and figures relating to the current Euro zone crisis now made familiar reading to Rachel

"Well if you can understand it perhaps you will be good enough to vet it for me so that you can ascertain whether I have made any boobs with what I have said. I guess I would hate to put it in front of the Council with a load of mistakes in it! They won't take the English serious enough as it is! In fact they already call us the little Englanders so if they find any mistakes we will also be known of as the thick Englanders"

Naturally this was only the completion of the first of many papers that he passed to her leaning over her shoulder in a somewhat anxious manner whilst she in turn scrutinised each one for any economic errors. On several occasions she was forced to draw his attention to a minor error which he was then able to correct.

"You are an absolute god send to me Rachel!" She was surprised for she had not expected thanks from this man. "Guess I would have been like a fish out of water without your assistance. I suppose if you must know this is not my usual job but it so happened that the powers that be decided that I had the gift of the gab on things that mattered and so I would be able to put across our own countries point of view on things that were important!" She didn't know why he had suddenly decided to confide matters relating to his work. All that she did know was that Callum, once one really got to know him, seemed to be a far nicer guy than what she had thought at first, especially now that he had adopted a little humility therefore his confession made her search all the harder for any false premise that had been included in this presentation. She had of course already realised that this must be for something of importance but as far as any details were concerned he had said not another thing.

Excusing herself halfway through the morning when Callum had declared that they needed a break and had ordered coffee for them, she picked up one of the daily ship's newspapers on the way to the ladies. The headline of this gave her something of a shock for although it was only a media report it stated once again that the Euro was facing oblivion and on the verge of a meltdown. Callum wore a serious expression when she took the paper back with her.

"Guess it's no small wonder then that the boss is eager to protect British interests in this field. Guess this European organisation has cost the country quite enough money already!"

They continued with the work and now Rachel felt all the more eager to ensure that all the quoted figures were correct. Finally at one o'clock Callum replaced all the files back into his document case.

"I consider that you deserve some lunch!" And so saying he pulled out his mobile. "No, not here on board ship for I consider that you deserve something better for all your effort!"

Rachel glanced down at the crop trousers she was wearing and following her eyes he read her thoughts. "Those will do fine for a working lunch. I've just ordered a car for us!"

If Rachel had previous thought that La Gomera was merely San Sebastian the capital, which to her eyes appeared to be more like a village, then she had never expected to see the scenery of La Gomera with its spectacular rocks and valleys not to mention the twisting narrow mountain roads that the taxi was forced to take. She looked puzzled as to where they were heading and Callum appeared delighted to see her childlike expression. "You needn't worry for the driver is quite used to negotiating the curves in this road. I'm planning on taking you to an Oasis anyway!"

Perhaps the word oasis was the best word to describe the Hotel Jardin Tecina, a golf resort situated on La Gomera's southern shore with its five restaurants and swimming pools to match! Although the place currently accommodated those with a reasonable handicap in golf and of all nationalities Rachel found that they were ushered into a lift inside of the cliff which led down to the Club Laurel, a beautiful restaurant by the sea where an a la carte menu was presented to them.

There were even more surprises ahead for her for Callum did not appear to be in too much of a hurry to depart from this place after they had finished lunch. She had fully expected him to have his mind set on returning to the ship with his thoughts still firmly fixed on the following day, but now he appeared to be quite content for them to wander around the gardens and soak up some of the beautiful sunshine that they had missed during the morning.

"I guess we can't afford to let this weather go without sampling it first. Who knows it could easily be raining tomorrow!" His winsome smile suddenly made him appear younger than his years especially now that he appeared to be so light hearted and that in spite of the challenge that still awaited him. He had never said exactly where or what time this supposed meeting was due to take place, merely intimated that he wanted her to accompany him both as his adviser, as far as the economics went, and his stenographer so that they would have a record of the events of this time.

Yet now seeing him sitting by the swimming pool and soaking up the afternoon sun as she watched the more energetic guests perform their quota of water aerobics all that seemed to be far into the future. Indeed the sun was already beginning to turn its eyes in a westerly direction when Callum almost reluctantly summoned the taxi again to take them back to the ship.

"Guess I know that we don't sail until eleven tonight but a thought occurred to me that we had better traverse those roads before darkness falls." Perhaps he sensed her reluctance to move for he suddenly leant across and placed a kiss on her temples. "And that is for being such a charming companion today and also this is in advance before your friend Brett Chaplain mussels in. By the way just for the record I claim the first dance after dinner tonight!"

She was surprised he had mentioned Brett at this time for after the other man had walked off the previous night she had seen nothing of him. Not of course that she had been given much chance to see him as she had been fully occupied with Callum and in all truth she had never thought of the man until Callum mentioned him by name. The thing that she pondered about now was whether Callum had suddenly had a change of heart towards her because he required her services for his forthcoming meeting or was the man actually genuine? After today Rachel now hoped that the answer would be definitely genuine!

Yet as much as she did not want the day to end it eventually had to happen and the next day dawned with apparent speed. It being only a short distance from San Sebastian in La Gomera the ship was able to dock in Tenerife quite early the next morning and Rachel's first impression was that the sunshine had completely gone and the rain clouds had re-appeared once more!

Callum's meeting was not scheduled until eleven o' clock that morning although he had already told her that the place was some distance from the port itself, quite close in fact to the El Corte Ingles.

"Not that it gives you any excuse to rush in there though!" He had joked at the time but on a more serious vein he had also said that because of his tenuous position he preferred not to draw attention to himself by arriving there by car.

"So do you want me to don my hiking boots then?" It seemed funny that she was now able to joke with him and at least it was with some satisfaction when she was able to draw a half smile on that otherwise serious face.

"Looking around it now appears that your old boyfriend has now found himself a new interest!" He nodded towards where Brett had suddenly loomed like the proverbial bad penny but now it did not appear that it was them that he was interested in but rather the person who was with him. Glancing at the woman Rachel suddenly remembered seeing her before for this was the woman who had been on the bus in Madeira, the girl with those nails that nobody could easily forget where the gist of the conversation with her escort at that time had included some reference to the Euro.

"Don't tell me that you are jealous after all?" Callum took in her expression with a cheeky grin.

"No, it just so happens that the person whom he is with I have seen before. The previous occasion was when I was on a bus touring the centre of the city In Madeira. The only thing was that the person she was with at that time seemed to be quite voluble in his sentiments concerning the Euro!"

Callum's expression changed. "Are you sure that you have got the right person?"

"Definitely I can tell her by her finger nails!"

"Well I suppose that is one way of identification. Not the traditional method I accept but at least one concedes that it is one approach!"

"Callum, are you being serious about this or not?"

"Of course I am. In fact this puts quite a different complexion on matters. Wish you had told me before!"

"I didn't know she was on board before!"

"Then we will just have to be on our guard which again is reason enough for us to walk off this boat as if we are tourists and nothing more!"

She nodded accepting his words although inside of her a peculiar fascination was growing as to what this matter was all about!

To anybody, apart that was from those people involved, the meeting would have been considered boring. The semi-circle of chairs with the speaker sitting opposite to his questioners reminded Rachel very much of one of the high profile enquiries that had recently been shown on the television back at home.

Her own position was sitting in a seat that was placed behind Callum for the purpose of taking notes of the proceedings which she would type up at a later stage. She supposed that this role would put her in quite an enviable role as far as other girls were concerned and she deliberately scanned the sea of faces that were now poised ready to ask questions of Callum. Furthermore by keeping an eye on her own script she had also to be ready to nudge him if he failed in his turn to ask the relevant questions issued from the others

It was as she glanced around at this sea of faces wondering which one would fire the first arrow and craned her neck in an attempt to put names to the various faces, that she suddenly stopped, pen in the air, as she recognised one of these people. It was indeed the man from off the bus in Madeira, the one who had been earnestly talking to the girl with the long fingernails who was currently on the ship. She leant forward in an attempt to catch Callum's attention and in the process a glass that was perched close to the edge of the table fell and shattered the pieces landing on the floor beneath their feet.

At least in the flurry that followed with the stewards moving en block to clear up the mess she was able to bend forward and get the message concerning her sighting across to Callum who in turn merely opened his eyes wide before nodding his head in acceptance of her sighting.

After that incident she had to admit that Callum did well during the next hour and a half before it was time to break for lunch and thinking back to what he had told her she was hardly surprised with the delivery he made that someone had already labelled him as having the gift of the gab.

They were almost ready to leave the building when the person she had signalled out suddenly fixed his eyes on her in a questioning manner. “Don’t I know you from somewhere Madame?” He phrased the words in broken English and now feeling at a loss as to how she should respond she shook her head.

“I don’t think you have seen her Pablo because the girl happens to be with me!” Callum had obviously judged the situation and had rushed to her rescue. “Believe it or not this is my girl Friday!” Rachel wondered if the man would be content with this explanation and at the same time she also remembered the girl who was now on the boat and who now appeared to have struck up a friendship with Brett.

“Of course you do realise that we will have to go all through this again tomorrow!” Rachel stopped in her tracks at these words, for no apparent reason she had thought that this was a one off. Callum judged her move. “Why, you didn’t really think that I was about to bundle you on a plane back to the U.K tonight did you? No as a matter of fact the three western most Islands, that is La Palma, La Gomera and Tenerife all come under the jurisdiction of one authority whilst their brothers in the East, that is to say Grand Canaria, Lanzarote and Fuerteventura come under Canton. Therefore it is impossible, without treading on someone’s corns, to hold court with one without the other. Besides I now feel that I need to spend a little more time in trying to get to know you Miss Burton. Therefore after due consideration I have decided that after Gran Canaria we might just as well take the opportunity to sail back to the U.K. rather than put up with the harrows of the airport! Still I must admit that I am a little puzzled about the man that you claimed to have seen on the bus as well as the girl with the long fingernails. What I want to know is how they happen to fit into the equation. Anyway it should prove quite interesting trying to find out!"

They had intended to stroll peacefully back to the ship so that Callum could leave his document case in relative safety but even as they passed through the dock gates they heard something of a commotion issuing forth from the gangway and this time it was Callum who wore a puzzled expression.

"------The male dancer, the one who was arrested in La Palma and taken from the ship. I am absolutely sure I have just spotted him trying to board again!"

Rachel looked in the direction he was pointing but did not see anything untoward. "Well I don't suppose he will still have a pass to get on board anyway. But it couldn't have been him, not if he is still in custody!"

There were no police around when they boarded and therefore they concluded that they had been mistaken. Instead it was Brett who was the one to greet them after they had passed through security and the scowl on that man's face was enough to convince them that something was afoot!

⋆ ⋆ ⋆ ⋆

Chapter Three

"Have you seen anything of Greta?" The question posed appeared pointed as well as being presented in a rather disagreeable manner almost indeed as if he was attempting to remind Rachel that her place was with him and not with Callum.

"Whatever makes you think we have seen her? We have only just come back on board for starters!"

Brett glanced at the document case Callum was carrying and a sneer touched his lips. "Oh that, I kind of forgot you were supposedly working but the truth of the matter is that Greta and I had arranged to go and explore the sights together!" He dismissed Callum's own mission out of hand for his own self-interests which appeared to be far more important to him at that time: Not of course that he didn't intimate to Rachel by the tone he adopted what she was missing by choosing not to accompany him ashore! "Anyway if you do happen to pass her will you tell her that I am waiting for her on deck four?"

By this time the lift had come down to the deck and Callum almost pushed Rachel inside for he had obviously heard enough from the other man, something that Rachel immediately sensed as he drummed his fingers impatiently against the call buttons once inside of that conveyance. Nevertheless as Callum's cabin was situated on a different deck to her own and he wanted to put the document case away in comparative safety he arranged to meet her in the Restaurant for a little late lunch.

"Guess I would have preferred to have taken you out somewhere instead whilst we were still ashore but in truth I didn't want those documents to be lying about for too long!" Now the man's mood appeared to have changed and he almost sounded apologetic about the matter leaving Rachel left to still wonder about the apparent change in their relationship.

This was something that Rachel had reason to think about even more during that afternoon when they strolled around to view the sights of the city, more especially when Callum stopped to purchase a watch for her at one of the well know jewellers in the main square.

"Just my way of expressing thanks for all your assistance in this endeavour!" He slipped it over her wrist with a smile. "Guess I couldn't have managed without you!"

"But matters are still not over yet, remember tomorrow!" She felt devoid of something to say to him in response, beyond the obligatory thank you, and consequently she then turned her mind onto having to go through the same procedure as she had today at their next port of call, but Callum had obviously got a different prospective on his mind.

"Today or what is left of it I guess I want to spend getting to know you a little better, something that I promised myself that I would do previously. Let's start off by taking a break in that café over there! I do believe they actually serve English tea!"

Once the tea and cakes were served Callum decided it was time to ask her about herself.

"There is nothing that is so very interesting to tell about me, not when compared to yourself!"

"Then allow me to be the judge of that. Doubtless you have a family somewhere?"

"Parents now living a life of semi-retirement in a Northern resort. I say semi for although my father has retired from teaching he will never give up work of some kind or another. I also have a married sister who now lives in America and a younger brother who is a complete pest!"

"Yet in spite of the distractions you still managed to get yourself to University?"

"Initially Dad insisted that I should go, but then of course he would with being a teacher, although in actual fact he was quite right for I enjoyed University life and after I managed to qualify I found a job with your own ex-tutor Eric! That was of course until one day a certain person engaged me on a job I knew little about. There you have my story what about your own?"

"I'm afraid that my story is nothing as spectacular as your own! I found myself being enlisted into the service when I managed to qualify, largely due to Eric's handling of me whilst I was still at University and I don't even have a brother whom I can call a damn nuisance! But recently I did happen to meet a certain girl and ever since that time I have been captivated and under her spell!" She watched as the breeze that had got up during the afternoon caught hold of a lock of his brown wavy hair and deposited it on his face. Thinking of faces however made her remember another person she had noticed that same morning.

"I meant to mention it before but when we were at the meeting this morning I noticed that the man you referred to as Pablo had a recent scar on his temple. I don't know whether it is significant or not but I am sure it wasn't there when I last spotted him in Madeira!"

"Do you never stop working?" He greeted her words with a laugh as he brushed his hair back as if he was trying to tame it. "Here I am trying to get to know a girl a little better and all she can think about is work. Maybe that is why I am falling for you Rachel Burton. Eric Taylor did say you were one in a million and now I am beginning to find out what he meant by that comment. Please don't tell me that there is someone else waiting in that Northern capital of yours?"

"No there is no one!" She made her confession seriously even though her head had started to spin as she began to realise just what the man in front of her now meant to her.

He bent across the table and kissed her lightly on the cheek, an acknowledgement that was acceptable in these climes. "The rest will come later I promise you but that will have to suffice in public!"

They moved from the café back out into the avenues of that place and this time Callum took her arm although for her own part Rachel did not know how her feet were managing to negotiate the floor. She was intoxicated but not with anything alcoholic, simply intoxicated with being here with this man.

The day was to continue in much the same vein for after returning to the ship they took in one of the shows and then danced together until quite late; neither of them now seeming particularly concerned about the meeting on the following day for as far as Callum was concerned the preparations for that meeting were complete. Yet it was the good night kiss on deck as the boat sailed out of Tenerife harbour that had Rachel returning to her cabin with her cheeks a pretty pink in their colouration.

She had hardly managed to get inside her cabin however when there was a knock on the door. It was late but thinking this must be Callum who needed to remind her of something Rachel answered it only to suffer something of a shock she saw Adri standing there. In truth since the occasion when they had been returning to the boat late that morning she had never given the Croatian another thought but by whatever means he had employed the man was certainly on board and what was more he wanted to speak to her. Once again she witnessed the haunted expression in his eyes even as she hesitated to open up any sort of conversation.

"Please you will excuse me Miss, but you are the one with the kind eyes and perhaps you will help Adri for without your help then Adri, he is lost!"

"I thought you had been arrested. How did you manage to get back on board then?" She wondered for a moment if her curiosity had got the better of her when in actuality she was well aware she should have summoned help at the sight of this apparition!"

"Perhaps the police, they knew better than the mistake they made and Adri you see, he still has friends, one of whom let him come on board. In all truth all that Adri wants is to clear his name and Adri wondered if the girl with the kind eyes if she would help him?"

"Why what did you want me to do?" She really did not know why she had allowed curiosity to get the better of her. She knew full well that perhaps this was one of her weaknesses but this in itself was no excuse for her action.

"The girl dancer in the show, the one they called Amy, she knows the person whom I now wish to meet. I wonder if you would speak to her for me?"

"But it is late and I would not know where to find her!"

"After the late show she goes to the Lido bar on deck eight for there is a disco there and she goes to show them how to dance. You will go there please and tell her that Adri has need of her help. If you do this for me then Adri will be very grateful for only in this way can Adri hope to clear his name. You see Adri was in love with Amy's friend, but then someone in the western group where Martha was a singer was jealous for he wanted the woman for himself!"

"And that was what you were rowing about the night I passed you on the stairs?" She knew full well that she should not be asking him such questions but then Rachel had an inbuilt spark of curiosity that was seldom satisfied.

"We rowed about this man yes. But when we rowed Adri did not kill the girl for the other man is also strong and he came along as I left her! Perhaps if I had not left her the way that I did then Martha would still be alive!"

"Then wait in the corridor at the forward end of the boat. People seldom use the staircase there and I will see what I can do!" Eric had once said that when Rachel made up her mind she seldom bothered to consider other matters. The dancer nodded in gratitude and then moved away with a fleetness of foot that was an added bonus in his profession and still wondering whether she was doing right Rachel made to catch the lift up to the disco floor.

Fortunately at this time of the night there were few people left about for most of them had retired after a day out on the town. The disco itself was on the point of closing for the hour was closer to one am the following morning than it was to midnight but this itself was a blessing because she was soon able to spot the girl from the show whom Adri had spoken about.

Much to her relief Amy listened to her story without giving anything away and then obligingly turned to make for the lift so that she could go down to meet the Croatian. Rachel would have followed except just as she was about to leave someone caught hold of her arm.

"So this is what you do when you have put lover boy to bed is it?" Looking up she saw Brett glaring at her and felt at least thankful that he had not heard the contents of her conversation. Neither was Brett there on his own for the girl he had called Greta was also present and now looked none too pleased that he had broken away from her in order to speak to Rachel.

"No, you see I used to be a girl guide and my mission is to try to help others in trouble!" She pushed away his arm for she wanted no fireworks from Greta. Besides after spending the day with Callum she did not want to tarnish the memory before the day had finished. "And now if you will excuse me for I believe that we will have to make an early start in the morning for the boat is only docked until four o'clock in Las Palmas!"

"I wonder if your new beau fully appreciates the talons of the cat he now favours? Perhaps someone ought to let him know how the woman will easily let him down given the slightest opportunity!"

He would have grabbed her again had not Greta called out almost as if she was in some sort of pain because he had left her and for once Rachel felt grateful for the other woman's presence. In fact she now ignored Brett as she shouted goodnight to his companion and then fled back to her cabin wondering if she had done the right thing in accepting this mission after all.

"Guess you look tired!" Callum was obviously concerned about her as they made to leave the ship in order to attend the convention the following morning. The words he uttered she supposed were not really surprising, considering that she had spent half of the night pacing up and down as she still wondered whether she had done the right thing not only in trying to help Adri, but also musing on the apparently tangled relationship that Brett appeared to have involved himself with, for the woman he called Greta was most definitely not what she first appeared. At least nothing had been said so far about Adri reappearance on the scene so she supposed that was a blessing in itself!

It was as they crossed the gangway onto the quayside that Rachel noticed that Greta was in front of them. Today however the woman was not with Brett. Instead there was someone else waiting for her at the other side of the terminal buildings. Callum exchanged glances with Rachel for as far as they knew Pablo had been left behind in Tenerife.

"Still I suppose one could say anything is possible." Callum frowned now deep in thought. "After all it is only a short trip across from that Island whether by ferry or by plane!" At least she supposed the man tried to reason logically, but Rachel's thoughts were still focussed on the time she had spotted Greta in the Lido bar late the night before. Still she determined that she would not say anything for to have done so she would then have had to reveal about seeing Adri. Thus for now at least, she just simply nodded in agreement

The meeting that day was to be held in the Edificios Insular in the Alta Vista area of the city which was not too far for them to have to walk and therefore Rachel and Callum arrived quite some time before his Inquisitors and thus had an opportunity to look around the place. The appearance of the city had seemed almost gracious to Rachel but then of course she knew they would have little time to view the place after the meeting this morning for the boat was due to sail away at four thirty that afternoon and therefore this would give them little opportunity to visit the promenade area. Nevertheless that their stay on this Island was intended to be brief appeared to be something that Callum admitted he was in favour of.

"Don't forget that after this morning our current task will be completed and therefore we will then have all the time in the world to relax not to mention get to know one another better on the cruise back to England. After all it hasn't been much of a cruise for you yet!"

She wanted to tell him that she didn't mind where they were at the time for being with him now was the most important thing for her but just at that moment she spied Greta and Pablo crossing the road in their direction.

"Surely the man can't be coming here. After all he said his party piece back in Tenerife so I doubt whether he has a voice with this gathering!" But attending the meeting was obviously the thing that Pablo intended to do, not only on his own but also with Greta dancing in attendance. The man in fact glanced at Callum as they passed into the Interior of the building and one could almost read the suggestion on his lips; that if Callum had his own stenographer by his side then he would have his own help as well although Rachel did wonder how the woman would manage to take notes with finger nails that were quite so long. Unless of course they had been false all along and she had peeled them off for the occasion. Still with her blond tresses now fastened back Pablo looked reasonably pleased with his acquisition.

The meeting itself passed in a similar mode to the one the day before except that during the closing stages it was Pablo himself who sought to question the little Englander. "It would be interesting to know Senor what gives your country the right to demand a seat at our financial meetings. After all if I might be so bold as to state that the U.K has sought to have no part in joining the common currency but simply views the member states as trading partners, then why does that country demand to have a place in our discourse on measures to rescue the common currency?"

"Simply because the state of the Euro and the threat of its collapse will affect all European nations and therefore we feel that we are entitled to have a say in matters that could have bearing our own financial market. You also forget that the U.K has already adopted drastic measures in order to repay our own debts and yet we are constantly now being bombarded with requests to apportion further funds to rescue others who may not have been quite so frugal as what we as a nation have ourselves endeavoured to be. Therefore our own populace is now beginning to question why they have to accept cuts in their standard of living merely to bail other nations, when they appear to have little intention of adopting the same levels of frugality as ourselves!"

Rachel glanced at the speaker appreciatively for he had managed this dissertation without notes but merely through his emotions at the time.

"But we were given to understand that your previous government was eager to join us. Perhaps they had a better vision of the future with a United Europe than what you have yourself!"

"The government that employs me joined the European Union only as a trading partner and not part of some gigantic air balloon that was destined to sooner or later deflate itself!"

Rachel saw the one called Pablo squirm a little in his seat and then wipe the sweat from off his brow. He was obviously ill pleased by the response he was getting from the little Englander and as if to support him Greta now gazed daggers drawn at the English contingent.

"Please forgive me Senor for stating the obvious, but is it not after all a truth that your government still seeks to have a place at the table of the Eurozone nations so that they can voice their support for the admission of Croatia into the economic Union?"

"If that is the reason why my government desire me to be present then I am afraid that they have not taken me into their confidence over the matter. There is however one thing that I find most unusual Senor and that is your own attendance at this place for I do believe you took the opportunity to pose your questions at our previous location?"

Whilst Rachel marvelled at her superior's tenacity in this matter the one called Pablo turned peuse in his facial colouration. "I would like to assure you Senor that I came here as a guest. Indeed I was requested to do so by my colleagues in this constituency!" There was a general murmuring of agreement amongst the delegates present and Callum realised that it was probably futile to persist with this argument any longer. With Rachel's help he had delivered the British statistics and had also voiced his country's general feeling to matters appertaining at this time in the Eurozone. Now all he desired to do was to finish the meeting and gain more time to spend with Rachel for there was something decidedly special about that girl with the fashionable bobbed hairstyle with hints of auburn tresses amidst its fair colouration. Yet Rachel for her part was still toying with the reference that had been made to Croatia desiring to join the European Union and a sudden notion passed into her thoughts.

In spite of her thoughts however it was Greta who stood up to face Rachel as they were about to leave. "So did you find out what you wanted last night?" It was a deliberate referral to her visit to the Lido lounge bar to seek out Amy. The only trouble was that Callum had also heard her comments and now it appeared that he wanted to know what the woman was talking about. Yet Rachel knew in her heart that she could not afford to have her secret wrested from her for she doubted whether Callum shared the same views on Adri's innocence as she did herself even if the man did happen to have come from Croatia the very country that had just been mentioned!

"Everything was completely satisfactory!" She felt forced to answer the girl in some way for the other was now stood now poised awaiting her answer and almost looked ready to strike. In fact she looked most disappointed at the words which Rachel uttered, almost as if she had expected a different response. Fortunately both Callum and Pablo were ready to move by this time and therefore their escorts had little time to exchange further words. Once they were outside of the building however Callum still held a question on his lips and Rachel sought to find a satisfactory answer that would not give Adri away. Even so when she did not immediately respond Callum at least had the tenacity to change the subject matter whether he was completely satisfied or not.

"I guess as the boat is making an early departure we have little time to see the sights here at least not this time around!"

His words made her heart pang for it was almost as if he was speaking as if there was to be a next time and yet she had failed to take him into her confidence! Rachel swallowed hard as she realised whether she wanted to or not she had to tell him about Adri.

"Before we go back to the ship there is something that I need to tell you!" She bit her lip as she spoke the words and Callum decided that at that moment she resembled a naughty schoolgirl who had been caught out smuggling sweets into the dormitory.

"In that case I am sure that we have time for another coffee before we go back to the ship after all!"

There was a bar close by and Callum waited until the coffee had been set on the table before he finally turned to face her and Rachel flushed up as she began her saga for now there was little point in her trying to conceal the truth any longer.

"Last night after I went back to my cabin I had a visitor!" He had waited expectantly for her to begin. Now she had a vision of his eyes opening wide at this remark, perhaps his first thoughts were that this visitor must have been Brett Chaplain and an expression of relief appeared pass across him when he realised this was not the case. "It was Adri. Please, before you say anything you must know that I have always thought that the man was innocent. How he escaped from custody I do not know, neither do I know how he managed to get onto the boat undetected although he did mention a friend, a crew member who had helped him. He came back in an attempt to clear his name for I believe he knew full well who committed the murder. Anyway perhaps because he realised that he had my sympathy in this matter he asked me if I would go up to the Lido Lounge where Amy, one of the singers on board ship was working at the Disco and ask her to meet him. That, I confess, is exactly what I did, but unfortunately the only fly in the ointment was the fact that Greta was already there with Brett. Consequently that accounts for her slighting reminder this morning!"

A silence elapsed when she finished her tale as Callum pondered over its contents. "Perhaps I should thank you for having the nerve to confide in me although I am afraid that I don't agree with what you did. Rightly or wrongly such an incident could draw attention to us and to our quest which is the last thing that we want to happen. The man is an arrested suspect Rachel and therefore it is up to the courts to decide whether he is innocent or guilty of the charges brought against him and you have no part to play in this matter!"

"Then are you suggesting that I should have summoned the master at arms when Adri knocked on my cabin door?"

"Sometimes one has to appear cruel to uphold the law. After all you should already know this in your line of work!"

Rachel fell into a disagreeable silence. Maybe Callum was right after all and she should not have listened to her senses which proclaimed that the man was innocent; on the other hand the fact that the man was a Croatian appeared now to be of more significance. Callum realised her mood and took her hand. "Unless you want me to I will not reveal your secret Rachel. For one thing I would hate to think that the woman who goes by the name of Greta could ever boast she had achieved some dissention between us and secondly even if I do not agree with you on this occasion I think far too much of your judgement to undermine your efforts. Mind you my silence will cost you for I am not beyond blackmail!" She looked at him wondering what was to come next. "You silly goose I mean blackmail in this sense!" He bent across to kiss her. "When we get back to the ship I will tell you exactly how you can redeem yourself!"

They saw Greta skulking ahead of them as they made their way back. This time however Pablo was not with her but at the time neither of them ever considered that they had seen the last of that fellow for if the man had a Portuguese passport and Rachel purported he had, having first made his acquaintance in Madeira, then the chances were that he would be in Lisbon when they arrived there!

Dancing close to Callum that night with the promise of another day at sea Rachel tried her best to forget all about Adri and the fact that he was a Croatian which she still felt had some bearing on the case, but possibly she wanted to forget Callum's obvious disapproval of her actions the previous night even more. For with his body close to her own and his masculine hormones percolating her senses she wanted nothing more than to be with him and certainly nothing more to think about either. Greta however obvious had different ideas for it was almost as if the woman could not bear to see the two of them close together. She herself was back with Brett at her side by this time but in fairness the latter was still sulking after being left behind earlier on that day instead of going ashore with her. Rachel could not help herself but feel a tinge of pity for the man, for he most definitely appeared to be a loser in everything he did. Nevertheless she did not consider that she warranted the scowl he aimed in her direction. Greta meantime had possibly in a literary sense now climbed out her cauldron and appeared ready to seize upon an opportunity to dish out some mischief. Moreover she found such an opportunity when Rachel disappeared towards the ladies.

"Well did your woman confess what she was doing in the Lido bar on her own at one o' clock this morning?" By this time Greta had found some excuse to leave

Brett's side and had moseyed over to where Callum was sitting.

Her words served to annoy Callum for whatever had happened he now wanted it to remain in the past. He had already had his say on the matter and therefore the last thing he now desired was outside interference. Besides there was now another matter he was pondering over, something that Rachel had said that had given him food for thought "As a matter of fact she did tell me. Apparently she had been asked to pass on a message to a girl who was working there and as she was doing a favour for someone it is not up to us to try to read more into the matter than that!"

"The girl she came to see was a friend of the one who was murdered as well as being a friend of the person who committed this crime!"

"You are suggesting that if this is the case and the girl was friendly with the victim then this does not entitle her to receive messages from whatever source?"

"And what if I was to suggest that the source was Adri himself?

"I would say that you were talking a load of gibberish. After all the man was arrested or have you forgotten?"

"And what if I was to tell you that the suspect escaped from custody and is now resident again here on the ship?"

"Perhaps it would be better if you sought to prove your words instead of casting aspersions without having any proof of what you are talking about!" Callum could feel his colour rising as he sought to protect Rachel whatever she might have done.

Realising that she was getting no further in her attempt to cause trouble between Callum and Rachel, Greta skulked away and made her way in same direction as what Rachel had done when she had disappeared earlier. It was perhaps an unfortunate meeting at the door of the place between the two women, for although Rachel stood to one side in order to let the other girl pass by Greta obviously had no intention of obliging her and instead stood facing her opponent close enough for Rachel to see the green colouration of her eyes that complemented the colour of her talons, which appeared to be drawn ready if necessary to do battle!

"You may think you've got away with it by using all your charms on that man but you are very much mistaken. In fact I will make sure that the entire boat hears of your complicity with criminals!" Now she drew her face close to Rachel's so that the other girl could even spy the lines that she had rapidly applied makeup to disguise. "What is more I have a perfect tool at my disposal for your ex-boyfriend certainly has no love left for you!" And thus saying these words Greta then waltzed away having apparently no use for the conveniences but had merely sought to catch Rachel there. Moreover once she returned to Brett Rachel observed the two of them deep in conversation and it was then that she realised that the onus of their conversation was none other than herself!

"This of course means that you can no longer remain silent about the matter!" Callum was serious when she returned to the table. Serious and annoyed too that this other woman had attempted to spoil what could have been an evening touched with romance for them. Yet he now deemed that the fact of the matter was that it was far better if Rachel now bit the bullet and reported the whole affair before it became common knowledge, for on board a ship, news of this kind had a habit of spreading as fast as any virus!

"But I gave my word!" Rachel possibly realised that her cry was futile even before the words had left her lips.

"Then perhaps one way around the situation would be for you to go and speak to this girl Amy, the one you went to see in the nightclub. Maybe she will be able to offer some solution to your problem for after all she is now also aware that the man is on board!"

Rachel nodded. She knew that Callum was trying his best to be helpful on a matter upon which he himself did not totally agree and she was thankful for his understanding. She looked again across the floor at Greta now smirking in her direction and stood up.

"Look do you want me to come with you?" Obviously Callum was concerned for her welfare but Rachel shook her head. It was unfair to involve him for he had other matters to think about and if his name became tied to this subject goodness only knew how his position would be effected.

"It is probably better if I went on my own. Not that I am not grateful for your offer but you have far too much to lose if your name gets embroiled in this matter!"

Callum stared at her for a moment before deciding that this girl was really something very special.

"Then I will give you fifteen minutes that is all and if you haven't managed to sort matters out by that time then I am definitely coming after you!"

From across the room Greta watched her quarry disappear with a gleam of satisfaction in her eyes. But then Greta had still not finished for the woman wasted no time in speaking to Brett who after a moment got up and followed Rachel out. Maybe Callum himself missed this manoeuvre for if he had noticed and realised that Brett was following the girl then he would probably have done something to stop him but quite unfortunately this was not to be!

Rachel had no trouble in finding Amy for at the time she was embroiled in one of the ships on board games, for as a hostess even with a fine singing voice she was also expected to undertake other duties especially during the daylight hours. Consequently she was forced to wait until a convenient time between games in order to be able to speak to her.

Still the girl obviously remembered her for she greeted Rachel with a smile. "Ah yes I do remember you. Adri said that you were the girl with the kind eyes!"

"I'm afraid that they will be unable to remain kind for much longer for my part in all of this appears to have been rumbled and therefore I will not be able to keep my silence for very much longer!"

The other girl greeted her words with a nod that possibly signified some sort of agreement. "I have spoken with Adri and I believe that I have made him realise that what he was attempting to do would not bring Martha back to life and therefore he would be better employed in voicing his suspicions about the other person to someone in responsibility rather than trying to wreak his own vengeance on the man. Perhaps because I was Martha's friend and perhaps because I knew just how much the two of them were in love and yet both met opposition to their relationship from their respective groups, I believe that Adri did listen to me and therefore we went to see the master at arms together. Naturally the man could do little to help at the time other than to place Adri in restrictive quarters but he nevertheless promised to investigate Adri's story for him. And that of course is what Adri wanted, someone in authority to listen to his side of the story so that the true killer of Martha could be identified. What was more Adri did say to me that when I saw you then I must say thank you to the lady with the kind eyes who had the patience to listen to his story and had taken risks to keep this matter to herself!"

Her words had obviously been well worth the wait and Rachel sighed with relief for now it appeared that she had been vindicated and the onus removed from off her shoulders. Of course the crew would not like this matter to become common knowledge and develop into tittle tattle around the boat. Therefore after expressing her thanks to Amy she turned to make her way back to Callum but she had hardly got as far as the door when she saw Brett approaching. Instead however of the word Brett, possibly trouble would have been a better word for her to use for she could see the spark of anger in his eyes even before he even got close. She cast a half smile in his direction and would have passed him by except for his hands that now reached out to grab her by the shoulders and stop her in her tracks.

"Not so fast my dear for I am left wondering what you have been up to this time around?"

She was tempted to tell him that it was none of his damned business but gauged that this was probably the wrong thing to say with the man in his present mood. Indeed she was wondering what she had ever seen in him during the early part of the voyage that had succeeded in tempting her to spend any time with him at all and then reflected that in actual fact it had been Brett who had foisted himself on her and not the other way around

"I'm afraid that I have someone to see at this time if you will please excuse me!" She tried to move but those hands still held firm, his fingers now biting into her flesh.

"My word you do seem to be a busy one nowadays. Now I suppose you are anxious to get back to lover boy, perhaps he has not yet realised what a little minx you are! Tell me when you decide to ditch him will the Croat be your next lover?"

She searched for words to say that could possibly throw him off track but before she could respond a further voice sounded out. "I was wondering where you had got to Rachel, guess your time is up!"

A look of positive hatred now flicked across Brett's eyes. "We were just having a conversation about old times and how our friend here likes to switch her emotions when a new pair of pants appears on the scene, even if the person concerned is not exactly kosher if you know what I mean!"

"I think I understand your mixed metaphors perfectly well and they sound just as twisted as what you are yourself. If you must know what she was doing Rachel had kindly volunteered to find something out for me and your name was not on the agenda!"

Perhaps it was Callum's curt tones that tipped Brett over the edge for the next moment she witnessed that his hands had left her shoulders whilst a fist propelled itself in Callum's direction knocking the other man sideways. Yet Callum appeared to quickly recover and moreover appeared ready to return the favour. Fearing the results Rachel realised that she had to step in if only for Callum's sake. After all it would not go down very well if the press got hold of a story about a diplomat brawling in this manner.

"Let's go Callum, after all we have better things to see than wasting time with this idiot!"

For a moment it appeared that Brett was about to retaliate but Rachel immediately linked Callum's arm to urge him away from the scene.

"Well after all it was hardly my fault!" At least her escort had the grace to look a little sheepish as they left the place. "For let's face it you had exceeded your time limit!"

"Coffee and I will tell you how I got on!" It seemed to be peculiar for her to now be assuming charge of the situation but then she had the distinct impression that Callum appreciated it. Over the refreshment she told him what had transpired with Amy and perhaps for the first time Callum appeared to be more satisfied with the affair.

"I suppose the only flies now remaining in the ointment are Brett and his lady friend then. She has already had a go at me when we were upstairs before she followed you to the female conservatory!" Her partner now spoke rather thoughtfully. "Maybe you were right all along with your suspicions centring on Pablo and Greta and they are seeking ways that they can now adopt in an attempt to scuttle the British attempt to throw some reason into this Eurozone crisis. As for your ex-friend Brett, well I guess he is simply a fall guy who Greta sees fit to manipulate into being her pet poodle!"

Callum's description of Brett as a pet poodle amused Rachel so that a smile broke out on her face, the first for the entire evening as a matter of fact and Callum took her hand tenderly. So much so that Rachel forgot about the initial warnings that Callum has given about Brett Chaplain, but then she presumed that these could wait at least for the time being.

"Guess I like it better when you smile, but there is more I want to tell you but I think not here!" He stood rising her to her feet. "You do realise that we will actually have a free day at sea tomorrow before we endeavour to enjoy the sights of Lisbon without any meetings. Not that we will have long to spend there, certainly not long enough, but I have already some idea of where I insist on taking you, always providing you prove yourself tonight!"

She followed him from the place without another word for already Greta and Brett had been pushed to the back of her mind as she determined that even that was far more than they deserved!

★ ★ ★ ★

Chapter Four

Perhaps the first impression one got of the the area surrounding the port at Lisbon appeared to make the city resemble a place that time had passed by. It had moreover had a glorious past with an Empire that had once stretched worldwide. That was of course until the outside world with its power struggles had changed the mood for such places. Yet if upon arrival one possessed such an initial impression this was to quickly change as one got to know the city better with its mixture of the old alongside of the new, the spectacular alongside of the functional and with those white marble often elaborated statues that stretched high up towards the heavens as if in glorification of a superior being, that it proudly presented!

Callum had previously mentioned to her that he had booked a table via the internet at the Ritz Four Seasons Hotel, an opulent place of residence which lay opposite to King Edward VII Park, where one could obtain views of the area which had been rebuilt after the earthquake, for a late lunch that day. Late that was because of the delayed arrival of the boat into that port. In truth perhaps Callum actually felt that he would have liked to have lingered for longer in this place especially with Rachel by his side and thus to have been able to enjoy a little of the opulent luxury of the place, but unfortunately the time factor, which is so often the case, had little consideration for his wishes because the ship was only in the port for the duration of the afternoon. Thus one of the major areas of derelict land that had been transformed into the world famous Oceanarium had to be reluctantly missed out on this visit for after Portugal had entered the EU in 1986 the pace of development had quickened! Thus once lunch was over and because Rachel had never seen the city he suggested to her, even as she scoffed her baked Alaska with some relish, that they would do well to take a coach for a tour of the remainder of the place, a tour which in addition to the sights of the city, then followed the coast road as far as the resort of Estoril, a place that the Portuguese themselves frequented especially when the weather was as good as it was today, and a place moreover that Rachel had previously only read about and never expected to see!

Walking together along the promenade there and watching the Portuguese at play during the afternoon sun it seemed to be only natural for Callum to slip his arm around her shoulders and as far as Rachel was concerned she did not object for this appeared to be a perfect day with a companion who already made her heart beat almost erratically. Indeed it was a day that she did not wish to end but alas time was not exactly on their side for already the clock was ticking away and soon it would be time to return to the ship

Of course such ventures seldom go according to plan for along with the coach they had also inherited a guide, a native of that city who was indeed very knowledgeable about the different aspects as well as the history of the place. She was indeed so knowledgeable that one soon got the impression that the woman must be programmed so that they had to stop and take note of every building and statue on route. Indeed it would have been easy to assimilate that if this woman had been in another place, such as being a programmed guide across Morecambe Bay, she would have continued to recite aspects of the surrounding scenery even if the tide had returned and she had found herself up to her ankles deep in quicksand and rapidly sinking down into the mud!

Nevertheless even if at one stage they were having qualms about getting back to the port before the boat sailed because of the traffic that now circumnavigated the roads because of the Portuguese at play, and the fact that the guide was determined to cram in at least one additional stop to marvel at the wonders of the purple cathedral, as well as the Black Horse Square that was actually green to lead to the confusion; and the Monument to the Discoveries on the River Bank, they both had to admit that the whole thing had been an enjoyable experience and far removed from the itinerary of the Conference Centres. Indeed thoughts of what had happened before with Brett and Greta had now completely disappeared from their minds and they had even forgotten the possibility of Pablo showing his face whilst they were here in port despite the fact that the man carried a Portuguese passport. The erosion of such memories were however short lived for it was as they finally returned to the port, just as the coach dropped them off, they spied Greta and Pablo alighting together from off one of the trams that negotiated the hills of the city. Yet in all truth it could not be said that either Greta or Pablo wore a pleasant expression on their face, so much so that Rachel and Callum looked at each other wondering what had gone wrong between the pair.

"I wonder what has happened between those two? In fact Greta has a face like a lemon." Callum bent across to whisper to her at the sight of them, yet their laughter was to be short lived. Indeed perhaps it was unfortunate that Pablo chose that moment to recognise Callum for in truth the diplomat with the Portuguese passport now seemed to be determined to wreak some sort of revenge, more especially after something his escort said when she also spotted the pair, for he appeared keen to promote an argument with the young representative from the U.K whether this was intended to impress his escort or not!

Rachel had no idea of what transpired between the two men because whilst Pablo apparently key-holed Callum, Greta herself was making a bee-line in Rachel's direction and even though the girl appeared to be now gushing by nature, after their previous encounter, all Rachel wanted to do was to get back onto the ship where she hoped some sanity at least prevailed! To make matters even worse the other girl persisted in following her and therefore once on board Rachel, now unwilling to wait for the lift less the woman caught up to her, made for the stairs towards the aft of the vessel.

Arriving at her cabin however she was then plagued with guilt at leaving Callum in that manner and after leaving it for a few minutes she therefore rang his cabin on the ship's internal telephone system. For a few seconds she waited hoping for a reply but there was none forthcoming and therefore Rachel replaced the telephone receiver whilst at the same time she wondered what had happened to him as a tinge of remorse for having left him seemed to envelop her.

For his part Callum was subsequently trying to decipher what the man, known of as Pablo, was doing here at the port. He knew that he held a Portuguese passport and therefore the fellow was entitled to be in this place but the fact that he was also present with Greta under whatever circumstances had served to fuel his imagination.

Pablo however had other thoughts on his mind for now it appeared, according to the morning news at least, that Italy was also on the point of requiring a substantial loan in an attempt to relieve its debt crisis and to Pablo's mind it seemed only fair that the English should be willing to cough up even more money in order to relieve this situation.

"And how do you propose that the U.K can find that amount of money? Please remember that we have recently had a debt crisis of our own and it is after all only through extreme prudence coupled with austerity measures, which is helping the finances of our country to withstand some of this Eurozone crisis. Don't forget we have already contributed to the Irish coffers for they are after all our nearest neighbour, that as well as paying our contributions to the Greek crisis. Our country can ill afford to do any more at the present time for already our disgruntled populace are planning industrial action on their pension reform!"

"Yet your country is still in Europe and you are saying that you are quite willing to allow another member state to fall into bankruptcy?"

"Perhaps they should try to abide by some of the strictures we have placed upon ourselves instead of expecting hand outs from others all the time to relieve them of a crisis they have brought upon themselves!"

"I suppose you have heard that the Germans and the French are holding meetings in secret in an attempt to create closer bonds which will exclude other member states and that will probably also exclude the English?" Callum considered that the speaker's tone had now adopted a more cynical note to it.

"Shall we get one thing clear?" Callum found his patience was beginning to run out for in truth all the fellow wanted to do was to follow Rachel back onto that boat. He had seen Greta make a dash to follow the girl and now he wanted to know what that woman was about. Nevertheless there was still this matter to settle with this tiresome little man. "Britain entered the common market in the first place in order to trade with other countries in the European Union. We most definitely did not envisage the formation of some super state. Indeed if the British public were given a choice at this moment they would consider opting out of Europe altogether, for if we face facts we appear to be now heading towards a certain super state in Europe. This is something that we had to face on two previous occasions in the last century and quite frankly we do not envisage meeting such a situation again, a situation fuelled by folk who pay little attention to what has happened in the past and which could easily happen again. Perhaps Angela Merkel's prediction a short time ago that such a situation could promote another war is not too far from the truth!"

"I intend to fly to London to speak with your superiors!" Callum did not know whether these words masked a threat or otherwise. Indeed he had very little time to respond for the next moment he was hit by a heavy blow on the back of his head and slumped down unconscious on the quay.

Still confined in her cabin and left to reminisce over the previous night that she had spent in this place with Callum and of the love that had surprised them both but which they had openly declared to one another, Rachel tried several times to contact Callum by telephone but received a negative response on each occasion. Yet even as she remembered his sweet breath when the man had later slept, she was conscious that the boat had now slipped its moorings and left the quay to presently negotiate the Tagus river and thus she was determined that the one whom she sought must now be somewhere safely back on board. Consequently she decided to wash and change ready for dinner, just in case he rang her, before she finally went to search for him to find out what was wrong.

Heading eventually for the lift she passed Greta in the companionway but now the woman appeared to have little to say except for apportioning Rachel a positive look of venom. But then Rachel felt she had more important things to see to in searching out Callum than to listen to any tirade the woman currently wished to launch into and therefore she allowed the moment to pass by without response.

Search as she would however she found no sign of Callum in any of the distinguished salons on board nor even out on the deck where a sail away party was still in full swing, and as she began to despair it was then that she found an unlikely ally in Brett.

"Well he can't have gone far on this craft and I have heard of no reports of anybody jumping ship!" Brett's own mood had definitely changed. It was as if by ditching his troublesome mouthpiece he had reverted back into being his old self again. Not only that but he was determined to prove himself to be most helpful to her and such was now the state of her mind that Rachel forgot the warning that Callum had previously muted about this person! Yet it now appeared that even with the two of them working together they could unearth no trace of the whereabouts of the English statesman. By this time it was approaching the hour of the evening meal yet Rachel did not feel like going into the Restaurant and it was Brett who then accompanied her to find a snack in the Palms café. It was as they shared a drink together that Brett suggested that she should go to Reception to see if they had any news of the missing man. This of course was exactly what Rachel did whilst still in fear and trepidation at what she would hear and Brett accompanied her mainly because she guessed, he now felt worried for her and the possible outcome of

Callum's whereabouts. Of course they had also yet to spot Greta, even though Rachel knew for a fact that she was on board, and therefore it was not without reason that she naturally wondered whether Brett would prove quite so supportive when that woman eventually turned up!

The reception staff appeared to be very serious and exchanged glances with one another when Rachel made her enquiries before they asked her to wait for a moment until a senior official was available to speak to her. Such a request did little to soothe away the thoughts that something was amiss which by this time had invaded her mind but she waited until a senior member of the staff appeared on their request.

"Could I ask you Ma'am if the gentleman you seek happens to be a relative?" Perhaps it was these words that made Rachel finally realise that something must have definitely happened and she was conscious of Brett's arm now gripping her own in support.

"As a matter of fact Callum Rothwell is my current employer!"

"Ah I see for we were initially under the impression that Mr Rothwell was travelling solo!"

"And does that fact bear any significance to my question? I was with him in Lisbon until we arrived back at the quay and now he is nowhere to be found on board this ship. Surely your records will show whether the man reported back with your card system!"

"We knew full well that one person had not reported back on board ship and then we had a message through our on shore agent that one of our passengers had met with an accident and had been taken to the local Clinic. This information we were of course required to receive before we could leave Lisbon even though it must be admitted that some of the passengers did report seeing an unconscious person on the quayside even before the ambulance arrived to remove this person!"

"Did you say an accident? But that is not possible for I was with Mr Rothwell all the time we were ashore in Lisbon. Indeed we came back to the ship together after circumnavigating the city on one of your excursions!" For once she was glad that Brett was there to support her for she sensed that her hands had started to tremble uncontrollably and Brett now judging the situation had put out his own hands to steady them..

"In that case did you board the vessel together and if so is it possible that Mr Rothwell went ashore again afterwards?"

"We were actually quite late back -------!" She stopped as she remembered that Callum had been speaking with that awful diplomat called Pablo and that she herself had come on board without him because she had wanted to get away from Greta. "I came on board but I actually left Callum speaking to someone on the quayside. I understood at the time that he was about to follow me!"

"Then it appears that he didn't I am afraid!"

"You mentioned a Clinic?"

"He was taken there after he was found unconscious on the quay, I believe I mentioned that some of the passengers saw the ambulance arrive. Anyway once he was taken to the nearby clinic we were then notified of the matter!" The officer now assumed that he had discharged his liabilities and therefore the meeting was now at an end and it was Brett who was the one to ask the final question before guiding Rachel away.

"And has anybody said how he now is and the extent of the damage he must have sustained?"

"As far as I know the man was taken to the hospital unconscious and he is now in a comatose state for which he is being treated. The injury was apparently sustained through a blow to the back of the head which I can hardly see happening if he was simply talking to someone. But although no one quite knows how he received that blow we have already been in touch with the hospital again and from what they have told us it appears that he is now responding to treatment. Therefore if you wish to learn more Ma'am, might I suggest that you phone the hospital for yourself?" He handed Rachel a card with the name and telephone number of the clinic on it and this apparently was the signal for her dismissal from the scene.

"Tell me what happened exactly?" For once Brett's face showed some concern as he attempted to ferret the whole of the story from out of her.

"I gather that you did not go ashore yourself in Lisbon?" Rachel could feel the tears of frustration stinging her eyes.

"No I felt that the time we were able to spend in the place was far too short for such activities. Greta went ashore for apparently she had some sort of a meeting to attend but I stayed on board and enjoyed the afternoon sun. Of course I might have felt differently about the situation if you had been available but then I have not seen much of you since that boss of yours came on board. Maybe I am wondering now why I am helping you to search for him!" He noticed the tears in her eyes. "Sorry, I didn't really mean that, what exactly does he do anyway and what is your role in all of this?"

"Callum is some sort of diplomat and he came to attend certain meetings relating to the present European crisis. Myself I am an accountant who is qualified in economics and therefore I was requested to go along to act as his backup girl on economic precision and also to act as a stenographer for him!"

"Then I cannot say that I envy you for the job you do but there again I suppose that if you are interested in economics--------! Still I suppose this occurrence has placed a different complexion on matters!"

"How do you mean?"

"Well if your boss is some sort of diplomat who has met with an unfortunate accident then questions about this matter could well be asked in high places!"

"I don't give a damn for the questions or the high places come to that; I just want to know if he is all right!"

"Ah so it is like that: Lucky man! But that is not going to put me off. Perhaps his absence, unfortunate or otherwise means that there is still a chance for me!"

"And I presumed that you had found a new love!" Rachel was now finding his persistence tiring.

"By that I presume you mean Greta? Guess she was someone to while away the time with whilst you were obviously otherwise occupied. But then Greta already has a boyfriend!"

"By the name of Pablo, yes I know!" Brett looked at her as she issued these words and for a moment she wondered whether she was confiding too much in this man. Not that she had ever sworn the official secrets act but she worried in case Callum would have preferred that she had made an effort to keep such knowledge to herself.

"Strange but I believe that the man from Portugal was also is some sort of diplomat!" Rachel breathed a sigh of relief for obviously Brett had not taken her up on her slackness of lip. "Tell me why did the pair of us have to cop for that type? After all we were enjoying ourselves quite peacefully before they decided to invade our lives when we started to pull into ports!" He grinned at her in the same manner as he had done when she had first met him and despite her inner anguish about Callum she believed that she now had at least one friend on the boat!

This new bond between them was something however that Greta strongly disapproved of and Rachel's first entanglement came after she had spent considerable time phoning ship to shore to the hospital to find out about Callum. This was unfortunately the only way that she could contact them for her own mobile proved to be stubborn whilst out at sea and all she received from her efforts via the ship to shore means was a curt 'satisfactory' from the other end after she had practically begged to hear about the man's condition.

"So you are no wiser after all your efforts?" At least Brett had the tenacity to look concerned about the matter although even he was stopped from saying any more with the appearance of Greta who had the look of a seasoned pro about her!

"Ah so there you are darling, I was wondering where you had got to!" She oozed charm in Brett's direction and venom in Rachel's both simultaneously. To give him credit Brett did appear to be a little embarrassed for after all this woman had thought little about standing him up when it so suited her purpose. Plus in addition he now felt as if he had got Rachel back. Maybe it was because she needed his help but what of it, for he had possessed certain feelings for the girl in the past. "Have you not found any more Croats to mother lately dear?" This of course was how Greta now greeted Rachel even though by this time she already knew that the dancer had now left the ship along with the real suspect.

"Sorry to disappoint you darling but I haven't really been looking for them for I have really been far too busy of late!" At least she knew that she had Brett's approval as she made to stand her ground.

"But of course I had forgotten that you have been acting as that man's little stenographer! Indeed I saw you fussing around for him whilst we were at that meeting!" Greta spoke disparagingly of Rachel's role with Callum as well as seizing the opportunity to remind her that she also had been in attendance that day, but by this time Rachel had gripped the bit between her teeth.

"Actually I thought that I saw you at one of the conferences in a similar role!"

"Of course you did, but the difference my dear is that I did not lose my friend, not in the way that you appear to have done or was it the case that he had finished with your services and decided that he would catch the plane back to your native country to avoid the tedium of the voyage?"

"Callum was involved in an accident!" Again it was Brett who chose to interrupt her flow but after casting him a glance that implied that his was not the place to intervene Greta again turned her spite on Rachel.

"How sad that is! Did you have to leave him behind then?"

"At present he is in a hospital in Lisbon and perhaps I consider that Rachel now deserves all the assistance she can get to face the voyage back home on her own!"

"Well I admit that she deserves something but then I cannot allow her to monopolise you all the time Brett otherwise what will poor little Greta do?" As her lips moved in a deliberate pout Rachel could not help but compare the woman's dress to that of the apparel that Pablo had worn on the quayside for doubtless the woman was attractive when compared with Pablo with his greying hair and the brash tie he had worn in an effort to make him appear younger, a tactic which had failed most markedly, especially when he had resorted to biting his finger nails in a mood of frustration when Greta had moved away. She had wondered what the two had been quarrelling about at the time but now Greta's words demanded some sort of retort!

"I wouldn't dream of monopolising anybody!" Rachel had grit her teeth.

"On the other hand I have just begged Rachel to attend the formal night with us for I consider under the circumstances it will do her good to get dressed up!" Brett's words now came as a complete surprise to Rachel for to her mind the only formal night she could think of was the one she had attended with Callum. On that occasion there had been music and a great deal of laughter. Tonight as far as she was concerned the mood of the occasion would provide a grimmer sort of solace. Maybe she would have received some comfort however if she had noted the horrified expression that had now appeared in Greta's eyes at the thought of them making a threesome but then at the time Rachel was not interested either in Greta or Brett, for her existence now appeared to have been placed on an acquired state of automation that required her to extend no feelings towards her companions

With her straight blonde hair scooped back off her face and her full lips painted a cherry red, Greta fingered the heavy necklace gracing her throat and wore an expression on her face of pure evil intent as she watched Brett and Rachel dance together after the evening meal. In actual fact Brett had practically forced Rachel to attend by arguing with her when she would have far rather have spent time alone, perhaps because he believed in his heart that this was the right thing to do under the circumstances. Greta however had no such circumspect and feeling somehow cheated out of her planned social evening with Brett a callous tongue persuaded the bitchy female to gather others around her to speak about the girl behind her back and to spread rumours in an attempt to implicate Rachel in the Adri affair.

Moreover having met with some measure of success in this area her next tack was to endeavour in the practise of sending coded messages to the other woman supposedly from this dancer and in truth there are none so blind than those who refuse to see the truth about such matters! Consequently Rachel found herself having to deal with even more despair as the woman had a tongue that was able to convince others of the girl's devious nature.

Thus through choice Rachel would have isolated herself in her cabin the following day for she felt that she had enough indeed to cope with other than silly accusations without a single jot of truth within them, but then her mind was set on getting back to the communications deck in an attempt to seek further news of Callum.

Yet again however her efforts in this field proved to be pointless for once more she was given little detail because she could not claim to be a relative. Moreover by this time, as the boat negotiated the Atlantic steering ever northward the sea had decided that the time was apt for it to act out a ballet of its own making and glancing over the side of the boat Rachel decided that such turmoil resembled a soul in torment. She had deliberately kept out of the way of her counterparts during the early part of the morning in order to try to assess the situation for herself, for each mile they travelled was taking her further and further away from the man she desired with all of her heart to be with and yet such a dream was an impossible reality.

One person she could contact however was Eric Taylor. After all he had known Callum since he was at University and perhaps now he was the one who could advise her, and tell her what she should do.

"You mean to say that you have lost my student. Now that I consider was rather careless of you!" Eric's response appeared to be jovial enough on the surface although Rachel did detect some of her own anxiety echoing alongside of his words.

"Yes but what can I do? I have tried to phone the Clinic where they took him but I cannot get a satisfactory answer!"

"Then the only thing you can do is to get back home on that ship of yours for as I understand matters there is little else you can do and I also believe that is what Callum would have expected you to do under the circumstances. I will try to make some enquiries for you from this end: Not that I am very hopeful but we will just have to see what transpires. Tell me did the conferences go all right?"

"As far as I know yes, at least I believe that Callum managed to get his point across in spite of some strong opposition from one Portuguese person I would hardly describe as charming!"

"By that I presume you are talking of the disreputable Pablo! Even so no doubt the ministry will be relieved to learn that Callum managed to put the English point of view forward at these conferences!"

"Perhaps I am still having difficulty in deciding what all of this is about?"

"Maybe you were not intended to know. After all, your task was hardly to define and stand up for British politics. You were supposed to leave such matters to the experts. Therefore my advice to you is to enjoy the rest of your journey home and leave politics to someone with better training than yourself and get back here as quickly as it is possible!"

Brett was waiting for her when she left the Internet room feeling more than a little dispirited. Perhaps she had been expecting too much from her boss. Maybe she had been expecting him to solve the quandary that was still besetting her. But that had obviously not been the case.

"Is everything O.K then?" By this time Brett had observed the expression on her face and realised that something was still bugging the girl. Still perhaps in his favour he was on his own for there was now no sign of Greta waiting to wrap her arms around him and claim him for herself with that insidious smile that she kept for such occasions

"As far as things went I suppose, although in truth my boss could throw no light on what could have happened to Callum. The only real thing of relevance that he did come up with was to decry Greta's Portuguese friend.

Moreover he seemed to know all about him for he actually called him disreputable. Tell me Brett who exactly is the man and how does he fit in with Greta?"

"Don't you think that I wish that I knew? All I know about him is when Greta stands me up whilst we are in port so that she can associate with him. According to what she says he employed her as a temporary secretary, although I must admit that I suspect from over hearing a conversation between them that the man is not Portuguese at all. At least not by birth that is! But what interest is the man to you?"

"Perhaps because he always seemed to be present at the conference Callum had to attend and what is more I actually left him talking or rather arguing with Callum when I left to board the boat, my reason at the time being because the female you favour appeared to have some bone to pick with me"

"So you now presume that it is Greta I favour? That is where you are entirely wrong Rachel. She simply cottoned on to me because we appeared to be two single people travelling on this cruise and that could be said to be a natural reaction! Now however I consider that you need a friend. Therefore perhaps we should try to seek a little light relief for the remainder of this voyage. At least it might help to take your mind off other things!"

Rachel looked at the speaker and decided that she could never understand this man. Yet she said nothing in reply for in the back of her mind the figure of the girl who resembled a Swede still remained. Brett however, having made up his mind that Rachel most certainly needed companionship on the journey back to the U.K remained adamant and thereupon set about seeking a host of distractions on board ship that might possibly placate the girl's mind, so much so that she herself began to push Greta to the back of her thoughts for in truth, perhaps it was fortunate but the woman now seemed to be conspicuous with her absence.

Rachel did not know how he managed it but the following morning Brett returned from the reception with a brighter expression on his face. "Perhaps I have now a little news that might help to placate you!" His words sounded mysterious as he marshalled her towards the coffee bar and waited until they were sat at a table before he broke the news to her. "I managed to finally get through to the Clinic and gain a little sense out of them. Apparently Callum was repatriated to the U.K. yesterday by air ambulance after the medics said that he was fit enough to travel. I'm sorry I couldn't persuade them to reveal more details but I suppose it is a step in the right direction!" He watched the expression change on her face and decided that this meant far more than all the thanks he could get for his endeavours.

"Are you sure? How did you manage to get any sense out of them unless you claimed that you were a relative? How is Callum then? Had he recovered consciousness before they moved him?"

"Hang on, one question at a time is all that I can answer I am afraid. In all truth they would reveal nothing apart from the fact that he had regained consciousness and therefore considered to be out of immediate danger although the stipulation was that he had to be transferred to a hospital in the U.K. As to why they actually told me this, well I suppose I can be persuasive at times and what was more I did tell a white lie by claiming to be his employer! Well, is silence all the thanks I get for attempting to settle your mind so that I can share a more cheerful disposition with you for the remainder of our time on board?"

"I'm sorry! I guess my silence is not enough!" She bent across the table and kissed him lightly on the forehead an action that appeared to please him. Not so however another form who had entered the bar area at the time for it was immediately obvious that Greta was not amused by this sort of behaviour! In Rachel's mind she almost visualised the girl sharpening up her talons ready for the affray that must surely follow, but Brett also noticing her entrance saw nothing else but the girl herself.

"Ah Greta do come and join us. We have just had some good news about Callum. Apparently he has now regained consciousness and is to be repatriated back to the U.K!"

"Really!" The word was spoken in an almost sneer like fashion. "Well I have news of my own. You see Pablo has just contacted me. He is also now in London attending a meeting but then he also told me something else. Apparently it was the Croatian who attacked your employer Miss Burton on the quayside in Lisbon. And that is the truth for Pablo witnessed it with his own eyes for he appeared from behind your friend whilst he and Pablo were still talking!" After issuing the words Greta stepped back in order to view the confusion she had caused and now relished watching!"

"But that was impossible, I saw him leaving the boat along with the other suspect to attend police questioning!"

"Nothing seems to be impossible for that villain especially when he find those gullible enough to help him. Don't forget he was taken from this boat by the police once before and then made a remarkable return only to be aided by those who should have known better. I wonder if your employer who was inevitably struck down realises the part you had to play in transporting the criminal to Lisbon in the first place?"

As Brett stood to interject now realising Rachel's dilemma, Greta silenced him with a wave of her hand. "No, for I have not yet finished. Perhaps under the circumstances Miss Burton you might feel inclined to go and inform your mutual friend from the disco, Amy, I believe that is her name, of what your combined actions have now achieved. I will not be mistaken for a fool Miss Burton for that is exactly what happened, am I not correct?"

If Rachel could have found the strength she would have physically have hit out at this woman and yet her mind still pondered upon the fate of Adri and whether this action had been indeed possible, for if Greta was right then she alone was the one responsible for Callum's assault. Yet even now a picture of the young dancer focussed itself in her mind and she realised that he could not possibly have done such a thing, for the picture she saw of him in her mind's eye was of one who was gentle and kind. Thus now unwilling to hear anymore verbiage from her protagonist Rachel made a rapid exit and was quite unaware of the smiles that greeted her action both from Greta and from Brett.

"So you think that she swallowed the story then?" Brett looked at the woman who was left behind with a hint of admiration in his eyes.

"Why not: Why should she not swallow the story. After all it is plausible enough? I doubt whether Callum Rostron will ever be able to say who or what hit him. Besides as a member of the I.M.F I thought that you were just as keen as what the rest of the Eurozone seventeen are in keeping Croatia out of the club. After all that country is hardly in any position to contribute into your fund that is supposed to be gathering in for a rainy day!" She giggled sardonically as she saw his face flush up. "Sorry Brett but sometimes your expressions read like an open book! But then of course you are not the problem at this moment are you? It is the British with their fair play for all attitude that sickens ones gullet, and it is the British who are currently exploiting this notion of theirs and trying to influence others as to the viability of Croatia for they have no love for the Euro as a currency anyway. In fact it surprises me that they do not want to revert to their stupid old pound shillings and pence monetary system and keep their two hundred and forty pennies to the pound!" She managed her final rendition with a sneer. "Well no doubt we will soon become aware of what happens to that little scheme of theirs!"

By this time Greta was convinced that her companion was in full agreement with her and therefore it was time to foster a smile in his direction for she cared little for Rachel's present state of mind.

Yet the other girl did not go to seek Amy out as she had anticipated that she would. Upon leaving the duo she had actually taken a few steps in the direction where she believed this girl to be before she had stopped herself with a reminder that whatever had happened in Lisbon was none of her doing! This was a matter that she had to come to terms with for herself!

★ ★ ★ ★

Chapter Five

Although initially Rachel had left the place in order to find Amy, once she finally arrived at the Lido lounge, where Amy was currently holding a line dancing class, the girl found that she had second thoughts on the matter as she reasoned that in all fairness what had transpired was not Amy's problem, for as far as she was aware the girl had not set eyes on Adri since he had left the ship.. In truth the young dancer had simply done her best to relieve the situation on one occasion, and as what had happened subsequently was not of her making it therefore now appeared to be quite unfair to involve her in the matter at this point. Therefore it was Amy who was the one to look at Rachel's presence questioningly as one certain dance reached its conclusion.

"Have you come to join us? I haven't seen you with this class before!" The woman held a questioning tone in her voice but at the same time she willingly extended a hand of friendship and encouragement in Rachel's direction.

"Sorry, I guess I wasn't thinking where I was heading. In actual fact I was making for the coffee bar when my feet seemed to lead me astray!"

"Wrong deck I'm afraid!" There was no note of animosity in the other person's voice. In fact the other girl's eyes almost danced in merriment at the thought of Rachel having chosen the wrong deck. "But I guess that I'm always eager to increase our numbers here. Are you sure you don't want to have a go before you leave?"

"Not this time but thank you anyway!" Rachel made good her escape. After what had happened she was more than eager to hide herself away for she had no wish to come into contact with either Brett or his female consort in the near future. In fact life often proved just how wrong one could be about certain people and that was the way things had materialised this time around.

Thus finally arriving back in her cabin she vowed that this was the place where she would spend the last days of the voyage. As it was possible to obtain room service and food delivered to her cabin she decided that it was quite unnecessary for her to now venture forth for meals and if Brett did take it into his head to call on her then she vowed she would now be unavailable. Even so the tenet of words that had passed between them was still reverberating in her ears and the thought that she could have been wrong about Adri all the time was a bitter enough pill to swallow, more especially if what Pablo had said was correct after all and Adri had been the one who had caused Callum's accident.

But why should the Croat have wanted to do such a thing? After all if the rest of the Pablo fable was correct then Britain was in support of Croatia entering the European Union. But then she remembered that Adri was a dancer and not a politician after all and therefore perhaps there was some other reason which had provoked him to act in this manner. Had he for instance presumed that it had been Callum who had given him away in the first place? But after seeing Adri and a companion taken away by the police earlier that day, she began to realise that this was not possible, for how on earth had the Croatian managed to escape the bonds of custody? But then of course she supposed that he had apparently managed to achieve such a feat earlier in the voyage. The answer to all of these questions appeared to be in one imponderable mess and attempting to distract herself from her thoughts Rachel switched on her cabin television to watch a video review of the voyage that was being put out by the photographers in the hope of achieving even more sales of their D.V.D. Not that she was really interested in the contents of the programme for she had merely switched it on as a means of distraction, but one thing that she did see caught her eye. The photographer had been filming the ship from the quayside in Lisbon and had caught the image of Pablo in his lens. Now the scar that had appeared on the side of his face showed up quite distinctively. Not that Rachel at the time paid too much heed to it for seeing the positioning of the photographer she was awaiting their own return to the ship with baited breath, hoping now against hope that the man on the camera had actually caught a glimpse of Callum's attacker and had managed to film the sequence of events. This however was not to be for the whole episode finished before they themselves arrived back at the port on their coach. Yet as she remembered back that when they arrived they had espied Greta and Pablo also arriving together she did wonder how the photographer had managed to film Pablo standing there beforehand unless of course it had been taken earlier on that day and he was there waiting for Greta to leave the ship in the first place!

Having now seen more than enough of Pablo and with the memory of recent events threatening to return she switched the appliance off and decided that she might possibly be better occupied in gathering together a few of her belongings to save doing it later on in the day for the luggage had been hallmarked to be placed outside of the cabins before the guests retired that night. Not that she had any intention of attending any of the last night's frivolities whether these came under the guise of the Captain's farewell cocktail party or the show that gave a reprise to all the artists who had been taking part on the stage during the voyage, for Rachel had resolved that this was her cabin until the following morning and here she would stay firmly entrenched with no reminders of the past days on board.

The thought that Brett might possibly be on the same coach returning to the Manchester area did not occur to her until the following morning. On that occasion all the passengers had to arise early and vacate their cabins as the ship navigated its way back into Southampton harbour. She had not seen anything of the man since she had left him with Greta and now the thought of having to travel north on the coach with him did little to stabilise her equilibrium.

Yet as things turned out this scenario was not to be for Brett Chaplain appeared conspicuous by his absence when the announcement came that their coach was ready for boarding and the passengers for it were now requested to proceed through passport control. Neither was he present on the journey back again to the North of England: Not that Rachel did not feel relieved at not seeing him, just merely curious as to what had happened to him.

Perhaps it was however his very absence that helped to lull her into a sleep like situation waking up only casually at the service stops and not fully regaining her composmentos until the coach was on the outskirts of Manchester, which was the first drop off point before the vehicle continued into Northern Lancashire. Thus she was to find herself practically without prior warning standing in the midst of the shopping centre alone with only her luggage for company. Still it was easy for her to summon a taxi from here and within a short time she arrived at her own front door and was applying the key to the lock.

Her first inclination was now to enjoy the solitude that this place brought her for surely it was far removed from the ardours of the past fortnight. Even so she knew that she ought to phone Eric and let him know that she had arrived back, therefore almost reluctantly she picked up the telephone. As by this time he would obviously have left the office precincts she took the option of phoning him at home.

"Ah Rachel! Guess it is good to hear your voice. Can I presume that you have now arrived home safely?

"I have just about, yes. I just wondered if you had heard anything about Callum?"

She sensed the voice pause at the other end of the line before Eric Taylor made his response to the question. "Perhaps that is something that we can discuss at the office tomorrow Rachel. At the moment I am sure that you must have plenty to do with your unpacking and anyway I want to hear all about your trip and whether you managed to master all that documentation in time for his Lordship--------!"

"But he has been hurt. I heard that he was being flown back to the U.K.-------!"

"Well I can assure you that he is not here camping under my bed at the moment. But as I have already said we will discuss the matter at the office in the morning for there is something else you need to know and I feel absolutely sure that you must be far too busy tonight for us to go into such details! Besides there are matters here that I need to attend to so whilst it is good to hear that you are home Rachel we will meet up at the office tomorrow morning!" The line went dead on her even as she was still holding onto it and Rachel was forced to place her thoughts and feelings into a holding position until the following day.

Whether sleep came easy to Rachel that night is a matter for conjecture but the following morning saw her ready to make her presence at the office quite early, even before Eric Taylor himself made an appearance. Of course there were others in the place who wanted to know details of her trip but Rachel kept her counsel on such matters apart from issuing the usual platitudes such as ‘yes I had a great time thank you’. Perhaps she was indeed fortunate that the others working at the place had no idea about the instructions she had been given beforehand or of the proposed meeting with Callum Rothwell, for Rachel at this point was trying very hard if unsuccessfully to push all such thoughts to the back of her mind.

At precisely nine o’clock, punctual as always, Eric Taylor entered the building to deposit his hat on the hat stand and after attending to the preliminaries, motioned Rachel to follow him into his office.

“I presume that you managed to conduct yourself in an appropriate manner Miss Burton. Did you manage to read the dossier that was left for you before you actually met Mr Rothwell and was the subsequent meeting that you attended to his satisfaction?”

“Mr Taylor you know full well that he was flown back to England after meeting with an unfortunate accident. Have you found out yet how the man is?” Rachel could contain her questions no longer for they seemed to burst forth out of her lips demanding to be heard and unwilling to be contained any further despite her boss’ own queries.

“Sit down Miss Burton!” The man beheld her figure through his horned rimmed spectacles before adjusting them on his face. ”In truth I have no idea how Mr Rothwell is at the present time, nor for that matter where he is except that his present location is somewhere in England. To enquire further about his health is not my brief, nor would questions of that nature be welcomed by his superiors. But your own position in this apparently long running saga appears to be a different matter for I have been given instructions that I have to hand this envelope and train warrant to you upon your return for apparently the selected ones based in the capital now wish to make your acquaintance. Why and what for I do not know for again it is an inconvenience to me to have to abide with you away from your desk any longer. But these people from the capital appear to have strong voices and therefore it is not up to either of us to argue about the matter or question their commands!"

"But I have only just returned from the south of the country!" Rachel almost wailed in a dispirited fashion. In truth she had expected Eric Taylor to have at least found out about Callum for her.

"I am afraid that whether you have just travelled back or not is of little consequence when the men in suits demand your presence Miss Burton, otherwise I would have argued against you leaving here if only from my own point of view. In the envelope you will find an address in London where you are to attend promptly at ten tomorrow morning and they have also provided you with overnight accommodation in one of the cities well known hotels for your trouble!"

So that was supposed to be her payment for going there, was it? Indeed if it had not been for Callum and the fact that she was probably more likely to find out how he was from this place than she was here back at home she would have point blankly refused to take the envelope her boss now held out. "And have you any idea what it is all about then Mr Taylor?"

"I am afraid that such people do not often take me into their confidence. No doubt they have reasons of their own Miss Burton. Therefore I would advise you to oblige them by getting there as quickly as it is possible for one does not offend such people by choice!"

She was dismissed from this meeting of that Rachel had no doubt when Eric Taylor turned to pick up some documents from off his table. Yet as she left his office she was quite unaware of the sympathetic look he cast at her retreating figure.

Perhaps the others in the place were surprised when she spoke to no one as she left. Maybe they even assumed that she had received the short end of Eric Taylor's tongue for some misdemeanour she had committed. Maybe the girl had even be dismissed over something, for glances were exchanged amongst her normal work associates but Rachel never noticed them for at the time she did not know whether to be surprised or angry at the fate that had befallen her, for she certainly had no real wish to go to London, at least not at that time even though she kept in mind the fact that this could possibly be the only way she could find out what had happened to Callum. The only trouble was that in doing so she would be missing yet another day working towards gaining her articles, the bestowing of which would be due in the very near future.

"Maybe it would have been better if I had been born a bird and then I would have possessed the wings to be able to fly on this journey!" Rachel ruminated to herself as the train determinedly trundled the track in its effort to break the speed record on route to London. "At least that way my limbs wouldn't be so stiff through travelling over the same distance two days in succession!"

Still her means of transport arrived in the capital well on schedule and the hotel she had been booked into was only a short distance from the railway station where she was finally deposited. In truth whoever it was who requested her presence had provided her with a luxurious habitation if only for one night and Rachel now craved to know who this person was. Still relaxing in that large scented bath before she ventured to take the evening meal provided for her went some way towards soothing these desires at least for the time being that was.

She was at the address signified promptly at ten the following morning by which time she was totally convinced that at last she would find out where Callum had been taken and how the man was. The place itself appeared to be inhabited by men all wearing charcoal grey suits and for a moment Rachel wondered if her own attire was suitable for such an occasion. Upon enquiring she was politely but immediately escorted up as flight of stairs and deposited outside of another door which was opened on her escort's command and then she found herself alone in a sort of ante chamber from where she could hear the sound of men talking within the inner sanctum.

Whether some signal had been given as to her arrival Rachel did not know but she found she had not long to wait before the door to the inner chamber opened and a man with slightly greying temples invited her to step inside. Despite previously hearing voices emitted from that room Rachel found that she was all alone in the place now with this person and tentatively wondered whether there was another entrance to this room where the people who had been here before her had dispersed through. Still her host appeared to have been gifted with an air of charm for he warmly shook her by the hand before asking her to sit down.

"It is good to be able to meet you at last Miss Burton and be able to put a face to a name that I have only previously heard about. The reason why I asked you to come here today was to thank you for all the good work you have done for this department in the recent past. I am speaking now of your attendance with Mr Rothwell at those conferences which should prove so beneficial to British interests in the future!"

"You speak of Mr Rothwell. Would it be in order for me to enquire how that person is after his ordeal and indeed where he is at this moment in time for I do not seem to possess any contact number?" She bit her lip as she forced the words from out of her mouth, for after all this was the only thing she had come here to find out.

"I am afraid that your work with Mr Rothwell has now been completed and therefore I now consider such information to be completely irrelevant Miss Burton. You may rest assured however that the man is recovering well from his ordeal after what I would describe as an unfortunate incident. Therefore I think you can safely leave such matters in our hands. The reason I requested you to attend today however was twofold. First of all I felt that we needed to show an appreciation of your efforts, but secondly and even more importantly in our eyes is the fact that we wish you to carry out another assignment for us!"

Rachel must have looked quite shocked for the other person, realising her bewildered expression, gave a half smile. "I can assure you Miss Burton that the assignment we now have in mind for you is not quite as tedious as spending a fortnight on a cruise ship trying to adapt yourself to the learning process of European law. The fact of the matter is that we have a visitor to our country who is in our midst at the moment. The man is due to accompany the Croatian delegation to Brussels in the near future but as he has arrived before his companions we wondered if you would take pity on the person and assist him in adapting to the ways of our capital for the next few days!"

"But my employer expects me only to be away from my desk for twenty four hours!" The significance of the fact that the man had said the stranger was a Croatian had still not gelled with her at the time for Rachel had once again reverted into the methodology of obtaining her forthcoming articles.

"I am sure that Eric Taylor will be most amenable to the suggestion if I phone him over the matter and I am equally sure that a person such as yourself would not object to spending a few days in the capital, all expenses paid of course. But perhaps I ought to introduce you to your charge during that time!" He rang a bell conveniently placed on his table and was rewarded with the entrance of a young man. Looking up at this person it was not however the stranger she had expected to see and Rachel gasped.

"May I introduce you to Mr Adri Restonavich, the Croatian that I was speaking about! But then of course you need no introduction for I believe that the two of you have met before. Indeed it was Mr Restonavich who requested your presence on this mission!"

"But you are a dancer!" Rachel spoke the first words that came into her head.

"I was a dancer at one time yes and the authorities in your country decided that one way by which I could possibly learn some of the British idiosyncrasies was to apply my previous talent on board one certain cruise ship where I was fortunate enough to meet one English person with such kind eyes that when your superior suggested that I should have an escort whilst I was in this city then I immediately thought of you!"

"But I understood that you had been ----------?"

"Arrested, is that what you were going to say Miss Burton. I admit that there was a certain altercation on board ship but then the police soon realised that I had diplomatic immunity being included in the forthcoming diplomatic core due to attend Brussels in the near future!"

"You speak of certain altercations Mr Restonavich? It would appear then that this tiresome cruise was not without its moments?" It was the man behind the desk who spoke yet upon this matter Rachel hardly deemed his mood to be serious.

"Upon that subject I wholeheartedly agree with you Sir!"

"But the girl who was murdered?" Rachel was now convinced that their host had sat back to enjoy this conversation and was now expecting them to fill him in with the details.

"I have said on many occasions that she did not die at my hands: A matter that some people find hard to digest. But to those who are familiar with the result of the post mortem on Martha's body they would also know that blood was found beneath the girls nails. Yet there was no cut on the girl's body, and she had lost no blood. Neither could it be said that the blood that was found was my own. Therefore it would appear that before she died Martha must have struggled with her attacker and possibly scratched him somewhere!"

"Do continue Mr Restonavich for I find this drama to be almost refreshing especially when compared with the status quo we are subjected to in Her Majesty's Service!"

Rachel closed her lips stubbornly at the listener's comments. True there were many more questions she wanted to ask the Croatian, especially when she thought yet again of that scar on Pablo's face, but not at the expense of providing entertainment for this other person whoever he thought he was. Maybe Adri realised something of the pattern of her thoughts at the time for he suddenly smiled and their host after establishing that he was going to be entertained no further regarded the pair in the light of his own work that needed completion.

"Your accommodation at the hotel has been extended Miss Burton for the rest of the week and a room at the place has also been booked for Mr Restonavich until he is able to re-join his delegation. Therefore perhaps you will now be good enough to escort Mr Restonavich there and afterwards seek to familiarise him with a few of our famous landmarks!"

This was their dismissal Rachel knew and yet she had still not found out the very thing she had ventured here for in the first place. "I'm afraid that my employer is expecting me to be back at my desk in Manchester tomorrow Sir!" At least she felt that she must raise some objection.

"Eric Taylor I believe you are talking about. Well there is no need to worry on that account Miss Burton for he will be contacted to inform him that we require your services for a while longer. Now if that is all ------- Oh of course I suppose you are worried about taking your articles. Well I can assure you that will be taken care of for you. Good day to you Miss Burton!"

Quite suddenly she found herself outside of that office door, which by now resembled something of a blockade, with Adri by her side. Perhaps the Croatian realised something of her thoughts for he smiled almost sympathetically in her direction. "Guess I seem to have landed you in it. If this is so then I apologise but you were the only person I could see befriending me in a foreign country even if it is only for a short duration!"

"I actually came here expecting to find out about Callum Rothwell!" Rachel was still dispirited at her failure in this quest.

"I only wish that I could help you, but if it is any consolation to you the man is alive and apparently he is now much better. No doubt he will be able to contact you himself soon!"

"I only hope that you are right!" By this time they had left the sombre building with its even more sombre inhabitants and crossed back again to the hotel so that Adri could sign in at the reception desk and collect his key. In truth she still had a wealth of questions to put to the Croatian for the words that Pablo had uttered about the Croatian being responsible for Callum's injuries still remained in her head even if she now felt that such thoughts were quite incredible!

It was after Adri had signed into the hotel and established himself in this place that the time for more questions became opportune and indeed it was Adri himself that ventured to open up this window of opportunity.

"Tell me Miss Burton do you believe that one can fall in love at first sight?" He surprised Rachel with his question for she in turn had been rapidly assimilating the contents of an almanac of the very places of interest in the Capital city, being quite unfamiliar with them herself, where she could begin her quest. "I felt that was the case between Martha and myself for we had not known each other for long, only for the duration of that voyage and yet I was positive that the girl provided my world!"

"You say that but shortly before she was killed I spotted the pair of you having what looked like a heated argument!"

"That is true and something that I cannot deny! Our squabble was about a man who was a musician in the troop that she was in. It was the same person who later accompanied me to the police station. At the time I admit that I fully believed that this person had killed my Martha in some sort of revenge attack for losing interest in him but in truth neither of us laid one finger on the poor girl. You cannot believe Miss Burton that I would have killed the person whom I loved?"

"I must admit that at the time I did have my suspicions although I did find it hard to believe that someone who displayed such a gentle nature as what you have yourself could prove to be so violent. But the police released you and therefore I presume they were satisfied as to your innocence?"

"They released both of us for as I explained when they examined Martha they discovered blood beneath her finger nails. Such blood belonged to neither of us and the police said that the blood must have been there because the girl put up some sort of fight against her attacker and probably in the process managed to scratch him!"

Again the vision of Pablo's face with that deep scratch mark on it came into view. "Maybe I now have some idea who committed this foul act after all!" She spoke the words in a whisper but the Croatian obviously heard her.

"You have then you will tell me so that Adri may reap his revenge on this person!"

"It is only a supposition on my part and in any case as the person concerned also happens to be a diplomat, although not from this country, you have your own position to consider!"

Her companion thought about this for a few seconds although he was obviously not totally convinced. "Then you will point out this person to me if we should meet him again!"

"I think that is highly unlikely!" Rachel spoke the words but at the same time remembered what Pablo had said about coming to London. Still she presumed that the city was large enough to hide a multitude of folk and it would be far better for her to now change the subject. "Take a look now at the London Eye!" She pointed in its direction but Adri had still not finished.

"The man whom you were with on the boat: I heard you asking questions about him. Why was that, did you lose him or something?"

"He met with an unfortunate accident before we left Lisbon. I haven't seen him since although I believe he was flown back to the U.K. Now however no one seems willing to say where he is!"

"Ah, the men in the grey suits, you mean? Adri does not know about such things: He only wishes that he could tell you. I think that maybe you liked the man. I saw you together and you looked comfortable-----is that the word? You will have to excuse my English I am afraid!"

"Your English is absolutely fine. I suppose that we were comfortable together although actually he was my boss on that cruise!"

"Ah I see. Those are the Houses of Parliament are they not?"

"Yes that is correct and beyond them is the clock which we call Big Ben!"

"I have seen it sometimes on the television back at home. So your boss was a diplomat too?"

"Sort of, we had to attend various meetings whilst we were abroad. But what is your own role in this delegation from Croatia?"

"It is but a minor role but I have to attend Brussels with them!" Adri was unwilling now to speak on the subject further so together they continued to tour the sights stopping only when they were tired with all the footwork and it was also time for a meal upon which point they returned to the hotel. Rachel's feelings for the day were that she may have had a charming companion but as yet she was no nearer in finding out what she needed to know. To add fuel to such feelings she received a call from Eric Taylor that same night.

"So apparently you are not after all coming straight back to Manchester if the call I received from London is anything to go by. The question is did you find out what you wanted to know before you allowed yourself to get roped into this further assignment?"

"I'm afraid not. Everyone around here seems to be so tight lipped about the matter!"

"Well that I am afraid is a hallmark of the Service. So how long do you expect that they will be keeping you as a good luck charm?"

"Apparently until the Croatian delegation arrive prior to them visiting Brussels. Until that time I appear to have been charged with looking after one of their number!"

"Babysitting will hardly be considered when you apply for your articles!"

"I know that. Fortunately I believe that it is only for a couple of days or so!"

"Then I hope for your sake that is the case. Perhaps you will phone me then when you are free to return?"

Rachel replaced the receiver feeling more than a little downcast. This was not what she wanted. Adri was a nice enough guy, she had obviously been quite wrong when she had made certain assumptions about him, but the sooner this delegation from Croatia arrived the better as far as she was concerned!

She was instructing Adri on the use of the tube at one of the stations on the following morning; a ridiculous task for her really for she herself had never ever been on that system before but she supposed that her English was at least better than his own in the interpretation of the signs and instructions. It was just at that moment when the figure of a certain person suddenly caught her eye and she stopped rather abruptly for she had not expected to have seen this person again.

Brett Chaplain was in the act of purchasing his own ticket when he suddenly turned and spotted her and naturally enough this proved to be enough excuse for him to make his way over to where they were currently standing. If he was surprised to see who her companion was Brett gave no inkling of this as he made his approach, instead he greeted her almost as if she was some long lost relative.

"Perhaps you are the last person I expected to see here Rachel. I understood that you had returned back to the North of the country?"

"I did, but now as you can see I am back again!" She refused to go into any details concerning her presence but noted that his eyes were now fixed questioningly on Adri. "Of course you will possibly remember Mr Restonavich. He is apparently one of those who are making up the number of Croatian delegates due to fly to Brussels shortly!" There was no secret in that at least and Brett could make out of it what he would.

"I see!" Rachel was rapidly under the impression that Brett did not really see at all for his eyes were still full of suspicion as he regarded her companion and concluded that the matter need further words of explanation from her. Not that she was inclined to provide any more detail concerning Adri's presence and instead she focussed her intent upon Brett himself.

"I could ask the question as to why your own presence is here in London at this time Mr Chaplain for I understood that you also lived further to the North of the country yourself?" She remembered then that she had not seen him on the returning coach, not that at the time she had any desire to do so but the fact was that he had been on that coach at the commencement of their voyage.

"I had some business to attend to first of all in the city!" He was obviously disinclined to provide further details and Rachel could not help but wonder whether this so called business included Greta. "Still apart from my obvious surprise it is quite delightful to see you Rachel. Maybe we ought to celebrate our meeting with a coffee or something?"

Rachel glanced in Adri's direction but her companion appeared to be quite au-fait with the idea and therefore she nodded in response. "Maybe it will provide a welcome rest for us after studying the inner workings of the Underground system!"

Brett opened his eyes wide at what she had said. "Then I sincerely hope that sabotage was not on your agenda Mr Restonavich?"

"Of course not!" It was Rachel who responded before the Croatian had a chance to reply. "Mr Restonavich is simply a visitor to our shores and therefore as well as requiring some degree of respect it was felt opportune for me to acquaint him with some of our more splendid sights. Don't forget he is only with us for a short time and therefore it was opportune to cram as many of the City sights as were available during his brief stay!"

She prided herself on her response although she still had the distinct feeling that Brett was not particularly at one with her words.

"One must concede that there are plenty of more interesting places to take our guest than the Tube system Miss Burton!"

"Maybe that is true enough but then if Mr Restonavich wishes to travel around during his stay in our capital then the Tube might possible be a good way for him to get about!" She preened herself at her words as they entered the coffee shop that Brett had already indicated, which appeared to be a place where Adri immediately felt at home.

"To get back to cases I was wondering whether you had traced the whereabouts of your former employer yet Miss Burton?" The coffee has been served when Brett issued forth his next question as Adri toyed with the sugar bowl helping himself to quite a liberal amount.

"I am afraid that the answer to your question is in the negative. I have heard however that he is now back in England and responding to treatment quite well and moreover I expect that once he has fully recovered he will be able to supply some of the missing answers to the conundrum!" And with that she took a sip from out of her coffee cup expressing a delight in the flavour of the liquid!"

"Then if you are part of this Croatian delegation that is due to land on our shores perhaps you could tell us exactly why you appear to be her in advance of your colleagues?" Brett's eyes flashed as he turned once again on the unsuspecting Croatian and Rachel could not help but wonder what the Englishman intended to get out of him!

"The answer to your question is quite simple Mr Chaplain for if you remember the cruise boat itself returned to these shores and therefore it was pointless for me to think of flying back to Croatia only to return back to this country with my colleagues!" The Croatian had abandoned ladling sugar into his coffee and now regarded his questioner with a pair of ice blue eyes. Indeed such items of refraction appeared so cold that they almost resembled some iceberg out in the mid-Atlantic and perhaps the idea did occur to Rachel that this man would have been quite capable of landing Callum that blow on the quayside in Lisbon. But then she dismissed the thought even as the Croatian returned to stirring his coffee, for the Adri that she remembered was not capable of such a trick.

"Strange, but I did not think that you returned with us to Southampton. I thought we left you and a friend talking to the police!" Brett was still hedging almost as if he was trying to arrive at some conclusion that did not exist.

"And of course you were quite right in your assumption Mr Chaplain for we did not return to this country by boat for your government kindly stepped in and flew us back to this country!" He spoke the words as if he did not care whether Brett believed them or not and possibly realising he had been defeated in his quest Brett turned his attention back onto Rachel.

"I did not see you disembark either Rachel. In fact I hadn't seen you since the previous day, don't tell me that you were in hiding?" Once again his words held almost a sneer like tone and Rachel remembered the warning that Callum had given about this man.

"That was possibly because you were far too busy yourself entertaining Greta!" Now finding the courage to stand up against him she was surprised to see Adri's look of approval in her direction.

"But that was only because you spurned my advances for in all truth we could have spent an excellent time on board, just the two of us together!"

"I think not Brett especially the way that things turned out and after all you found your consolation prize!" She gulped down her coffee now anxious for Adri to do the same so that they could escape from this place. It was as she waited for him to follow her lead that Rachel glanced out of the window into the street outside and then clenched her teeth as she spotted yet another figure that she recognised. For there was no mistaking the one with those long finger nails who at the time was pacing up and down behaving almost as if she had been stood up and that such an action was not something that she was accustomed to!

Chapter Six

Adri had obviously noted the expression on Rachel's face when she spotted the apparition for he immediately showed concern. Nevertheless Rachel had obviously not been the only person to see this creature for Brett had in turn stood and made his excuses.

"Sorry I guess I forgot something that I need to see to, please will you excuse me?" It was a trifling excuse but even so Rachel for one, was glad to see the back of him.

Perhaps the Croatian heard her sigh of relief when the man left them for that was when he looked in Rachel's direction as if coveting some explanation.

"I guess if Brett had not left to attend to matters then you and I would be leaving here with you shielding me from being noticed!" Her words were expounded as if in some sort of relief that her immediate problem now appeared to have been solved.

"Then tell me what it was that upset you so. You did not enjoy the man's company?"

"Not really I admit although I suppose I could have tolerated his presence for a while longer. It was just that I thought I saw someone in the street and quite obviously I was not on my own in thinking this!"

"Yet there was a time when you appeared to be friendly with this man when you were on board ship?" Adri's curiosity had nevertheless not been quelled.

"There was a time yes that I admit, that was however until he found himself a new companion more to his liking!"

"Ah now you speak of the one who was most forceful in her manner? So you are now saying that you believe that the woman is here in this city?"

"I thought that it was possibly my imagination for the light can behave with trickery on your sight, but then Brett obviously witnessed the same sight as what I did, which means that I can now experience a sense of freedom in the fact that he apparently went after her!"

"Freedom?" Obviously this was an expression that Adri found difficult to understand.

"Yes in the sense that if this person did exist other than in my imagination then Brett will be on hand to play court to her. For meeting that woman is the last thing I wish to do at this moment in time!"

"That remark then leads me to believe that there was no love between you?"

"There wasn't! But please let us forget all about the incident for there is still far too much to show you in this city than to be bothered about that female and one supposes that London after all is a large enough place to accommodate the two of us!"

"Perhaps tonight we will go and see a show. I have heard that the London shows are a must for any visitor!" He was changing the subject Rachel deemed quite deliberately, possibly to lighten her mood and she had to smile and nod her head in acceptance for after all, in all fairness she had to admit that her feelings for Greta had nothing at all to do with Adri.

"So have you any idea which show you would like to see?" Visiting one of the shows in London was possibly the last thing on her mind at the time, but then she had been employed to make the visitor's enforced stay as enjoyable as possible.

"Yes it is called the Mousetrap. I believe that this show has been showing for a long time in London and everyone who visits it is sworn to secrecy about its ending!"

Rachel smiled despite her own immediate feelings for this was not one of the shows she would have chosen by choice. But then after all Adri was a guest and her brief was to show him the things he wanted to see during his stay here. "Then we will see if we can get tickets for tonight's performance. Until we manage to get our hands on them though I am promising nothing for the show itself is still very popular even after all this time."

She supposed that they were fortunate in being able to manage to purchase two seats. Maybe it was because it was that particular night of the week, but the evening saw them sitting in the stalls together as the drama unfolded and against her better judgement Rachel actually found that she enjoyed it even if Adri insisted on buying popcorn before the show started, a commodity that she absolutely abhorred.

It was as they made to return to the hotel from the theatre that the pair came across that female predator again or rather came face to face with her in the street outside. To Rachel's mind the woman could have been cast as one of the cats in the show of that name for even as she drew close to them Rachel could sense that her talons had been drawn up ready to cause mischief.

"My word you are the last two people I expected to see walking the streets here. And together as well, although Brett did mention that he had seen you earlier on in the day! It appears that you have been to see the show, the one with the title I consider most apt for your situation! Still considering all that has happened I would hardly have expected to have found the two of you together. Tell me Croatian how did you manage to escape from custody and get to this country? I must admit that with you here on the scene London does not appear to be quite as safe as I had previously envisaged!"

"For your information Mr Restonavich happens to be a diplomat who is at the moment awaiting for his delegation to arrive in this country!"

"I see. Now of course that makes me wonder, does your countrymen condone such acts of violence that you have been capable of?"

Rachel felt Adri's muscles beginning to tense and much as she did not want to speak to the woman she realised that she had to defuse the situation. "Did Brett not tell you then? Adri was cleared of all such charges that were levied against him and not only because he had diplomatic immunity but also because he was innocent!"

"My, my! Now I wonder what your boyfriend would have to say about you championing the cause of those you presume to be less fortunate. How is he by the way? I heard that he took a rather nasty beating whilst still in Lisbon!"

"Callum is doing nicely thank you for your enquiries!" Rachel refused to admit the trauma she was currently going through puzzling about the guy and Greta in response sniffed for good measure as if indicating that she really did not believe a word she was hearing but was rather following her own interpretation that the pair were attempting to fabricate the truth.

"Then no doubt that is something to be grateful for although at the same time he will obviously have something to say about you running around with this err--- diplomat when he finds out about it of course!"

"Personally I do not think so. And now if you will excuse me we need to be getting back to the hotel in case Adri has had any messages from the rest of his delegation!"

"But of course. Still it has been nice to see you again Miss Burton!"

The woman watched them leave as Rachel hustled Adri back in the direction of the hotel. Fortunately for Rachel at least they did not hear the coarse laughter that emitted from the woman's lips as they departed. The meeting however failed into insignificance when upon their arrival back at the place a message awaited Adri informing him that the members of his delegation were due to arrive at Heathrow the following day. For a brief moment she almost thought the man looked disappointed.

"But this is good news for you isn't it?" Rachel was surprised by his expression for with this news her own departure for home now appeared to be much closer.

"This is of course what I am expected to do for the sake of my country, therefore in that sense perhaps the news is good. On the other hand there are still many sights in London that I have not seen and I would have liked to have kept my escort for longer!"

"Then you will have to return as a visitor sometime in the future!"

"And if I did would you be willing to act as my escort again?"

"That all depends on what I happen to do doing at the time. That I am afraid is the only answer that I can give to you!"

"Then I consider that to be sad. But this place where the plane will land, this Heathrow, you will take me there to meet my colleagues?"

"Of course if you want me to!" Rachel wasn't really thinking straight when she gave him her response for her mind was already toying with the idea on informing the Service of this outcome if they did not already know and then returning back to Manchester. After all, as far as she was concerned, her articles were still at stake!"

"I think you are now dreaming of returning to that place in another part of your beautiful country where you have some work attachment!" Adri now looked almost despondent and almost without thinking Rachel squeezed him by the hand.

"Whilst it is true that I have to return there as quickly as possible I will still take you to meet your colleagues tomorrow for after that you will have no further use of me!"

"But that of course is not true for you are good for Adri!" He bent forward to lift her hand to his lips and Rachel prayed that the man was not falling for her. Theirs was a working relationship and nothing more. Still she determined to let this gentle stranger down quietly and wondered why she had ever doubted the man's integrity for Adri was but a gentle giant and had not been born to harm anyone

There was almost a tinge of sadness in her heart when she travelled to Heathrow with Adri on the following day. A matter that in her eyes was totally irrelevant for surely as soon as she managed to deposit Adri with his colleagues then her task here would be completed and she could then return home back to Manchester and the chores that awaited her. Therefore she chided herself upon such thoughts for Adri appeared keen enough to meet up with his fellow diplomats even if, as the men finally cleared customs and made their appearance through the Arrival gate he did pause for one second to squeeze her hand as if to express his grateful thanks for all that she had done to help him.

A fleet of cars awaited the diplomats to transport them back into the city and Rachel watched them leave, a group of eager young men with Adri amongst them, before she turned herself to make her own way back to collect her belongings from the hotel even if in her case it was the train that was to transport her back to her destined location and not any executive car.

It was as she was leaving the Terminal buildings that Rachel suddenly came face to face with another spectre of the past however and in turn she must have gripped her bag tightly at the sight of Pablo barring her step.

"Now why is it that you look so shocked my dear? I believe that I already told you that I intended to travel to London myself. Therefore what better place for a meeting can you imagine than the complex of an airport where my plane has just made a landing from the skies above!" He ignored her reticence; in fact she was positive that he enjoyed observing her discomfort at seeing him again. "But I do believe you are here to witness the arrival of the Croatian delegation? A fine body of young men they appear too, such a pity that their quest is doomed for failure. Tell me though was I right in presuming that I spotted the young renegade who goes under the name of Adri amongst their number?"

"I presume that you already know that to be a truth otherwise I doubt whether you would have asked such a question!"

"So if it is not impertinent of me to enquire what made you come here today for?"

"I could consider it to be gross impertinence on your part for I was merely working under instructions. Still I admit that I am curious to hear why you yourself chose to visit the place at this time!"

"I thought that I had already made my position clear. I informed you that I would be visiting your city in the not too distant future!" His face bore a rather sardonic smile as he issued the words and Rachel's eyes were once more drawn to the by now healing scar on his temple which had the ability to flare up when the man was angry. "But of course I forgot to enquire how your boyfriend is doing now that he is back on home soil?"

"As far as I have been informed Callum Rothwell is now doing quite nicely. No thanks of course to the fiend who decided to fell him on that quayside!"

"Ah yes the tragedy of the voyage one must presume. And yet the one who committed this crime now appears to be running fancy free in the London area!"

"I wouldn't exactly say that for Adri just happens to be part of the Croatian mission whom you have just witnessed arriving!"

"Ah but of course. Not that I think their efforts will be any other but doomed to failure in this quest for I doubt if the Eurozone is in any position to take any new country to its bosom in the current economic climate!"

She objected to the tone in the other's voice and rapidly sought the means to make her exit from this scene. In truth a goodly proportion of her wanted to speak of this man's presence to the men in the charcoal grey suits but then no doubt they would argue that Pablo Capello was after all a European citizen and therefore reserved the right to be able to travel between the European countries in relative freedom. Besides even if she suspected the man and his motives she had no real proof to offer to back up any such argument. Still she was not for leaving the scene without one final verbal assault on this person.

"I believe that your stenographer is also in town at the moment. I happened to run into her whilst I was having coffee with Brett Chaplain ------!"

"Then that man is also here?" Rachel prided herself for she had obviously hit on the right nerve for the man's expression changed and suddenly became excessively ugly.

"But of course he is after all an Englishman and therefore this is his native country. But now I am afraid that I must be getting back for I have fulfilled my own duty in this field and therefore I will have to ask you to excuse me!"

The words she uttered were perhaps more wishful thinking than anything else but nevertheless they served to take the other by surprise and thus seizing the opportunity Rachel made good her escape. In so doing she still had something of a guilt complex at not reporting her feelings over this person, but then in the current circumstances who would listen to her words with any credence

She was still thinking on these matters and also haunted by the thought of that scar and how Pablo had managed to sustain it when she finally arrived back in Manchester. Whether Eric Taylor was actually pleased to see her though was a matter for conjecture for upon reporting back to the office it was a pair of shrewd eyes that met her own.

"So can I take it that you are now back here for good this time?" His eyes met her own with an inscrutable expression in them.

"I believe that is correct!"

"And yet I receive a phone message from London stating that you never reported back to them when you had finished your latest assignment?"

"The time was not exactly opportune; also the city appeared to becoming rather overrun with folk whom I considered to be undesirables. I did not consider that reporting such a matter to my superiors would be taken seriously and therefore I did the next best thing, I left the Metropolis and returned back to Manchester. To me that appeared to be the simplest solution to my problem. Not that I gained any insight as to the whereabouts of Callum whilst I was at that place, merely pleasantries that the man was doing very nicely, thank you and goodbye to that topic!"

"And would it help if I told you that the man in question has recovered enough to travel to Brussels? Apparently there is some important conference approaching and out own prime minister will be in attendance!"

"Then I can only say that I am relieved to hear it!" Her words were spoken almost automatically and at the time she never thought to query how Eric Taylor knew.

"Under the circumstances I guess he would not have been allowed to contact you beforehand and obviously his superiors also considered that to be an unwise step. But then if he was able to travel to Brussels then at least the man can hardly be considered to have been at death's door!"

Rachel fell silent for she had been positive that Callum would have tried to have contacted her if he had been able. "Now you are back however you will find a great deal of work on your table that has been awaiting your return. So perhaps I might suggest that you start by looking into such matters and put away any other far-fetched nonsense you might be harbouring?"

There seemed to be little point in arguing with the other man and thus Rachel returned to her office and now tried to push all other reasoning to the back of her mind!

It was the following morning that Eric Taylor handed her that impressive looking envelope. Not that Rachel had any doubt of what it contained even before she opened it and whilst she held the envelope in her hand she was conscious of her junior, a young graduate apprentice positively sniggering in her direction for this person too was waiting to attend the Board but unlike Rachel he had obviously found the time to study in recent days.

"It is your invitation to attend the Board at the University on Thursday of this week!" Eric filled her in with the details even before she opened the correspondence. "I can only hope that you have managed to put enough study in to impress them for as a group they will be satisfied with little less than perfection!"

Rachel thought of all the time she had spent in recent weeks studying European law and doubted very much that this illustrious gathering would hardly be impressed with that in her position. Thursday was only three days away and the studies she had recently neglected where piled up making it impossible for her to get through in the time allowed. To make matters worse the young pretender in the office was positively gloating for although he was of a junior ranking Ian had obviously put in the amount of work required.

"Is there any chance of postponing it? Would it not be possible for me to attend the board the next time around?" She supposed she was positively pleading with the man and was rewarded with a rant of juvenile laughter that put her request to scorn.

"I'm afraid that is not done Rachel, one does not attempt to put off the examining body until a later date. Such things are just not done. But after all you were warned that this examination was imminent. I know that you have had other matters on your mind but surely you could have set aside some time to devote to your learning pattern in this field!"

"But it was you who agreed to my going as Callum Rothwell's girl Friday in the first place!"

"I admit that I found my hands tied over that matter. Yet from what you have told me you appear to have devoted all your time to a cause that was quite outside of your brief. Therefore my only suggestion is that you now burn the midnight oil for the next few nights and simply hope that fortune favours you!"

"I have been very diligent with my studies!" It was that over grown school boy again and Rachel wished that someone would apply a gag to silence him. "Never mind Rachel after I have been in to see the board then I will wait around to catch the pieces when you are kicked out!"

At least these comments were like a whip that geared her into action. So be it, the next few days would be spent in trying to assimilate some of the figures which appeared to have gone astray in her head, for there was no doubt that this young imbecile had at least some practical use if it was only to gear her determinedly into action!

Thursday came soon enough and it was a rather wan Rachel who made her way to the university campus still reciting some of the documentation she had absorbed and trying to commit it to memory. Upon her arrival she was shown into an ante chamber there to await her moment of execution for the whole place reminded her of the precincts to a court room where no doubt she would be proved to be guilty as charged. Ian the boy from the office had been inside the inner sanctum before her and he emerged all smiles. Whether this was because he had confounded the board with his acquired knowledge or whether it was a show of strength against her own predicament she did not know. Nor did she have little time to ponder on the matter for having dispensed with Ian a man appeared at the door of the inner sanctum and called her name in language that exported something of a flattened tone. Perhaps, she mused they already had considered her to be a potential failure!

Following her escort into that room Rachel was quite convinced that her shoes were sticking to the floor and indeed if it had not been for Eric and the obvious trust he had placed in her she would probably at that stage turned tail and fled! To start with she did not really regard the board as people but merely robots who had been tuned up to pick her brains and it was only after one or two faltering answers that she finally looked up to see who she was addressing. After all someone had once said that it is far better to look the enemy in the eye.

Yet it was upon scanning this sea of faces, which at the best provided little comfort to her that her eyes paused on a very familiar shape and for a moment she began to wonder whether she had come to the right place after all. For sitting regarding her almost quizzically there could be no mistaking the figure of Greta Sylvio for even her long finger nails were gracing the top of the table where she sat.

The questions were pertinent by their very nature and to Rachel's mind bore little resemblance to the manuscripts she had endeavoured to study before this meeting. There were enough indeed to make her leave that barrage of questioning some thirty minutes later feeling like an abject failure. To make matters worse Ian had been waiting to hear how she had got on the excitement of having had an excellent board himself still manifested about his features.

"So how did you get on?" She wondered whether his question was strictly relevant for anyone could see from her face that she had not got on at all. Still something innate within her refused to allow her to admit defeat, certainly not in the presence of that young whipper-snapper.

"I am afraid that we will have to wait and see for after all the board still have other candidates to interview!"

"That I presume means you believe you didn't get on very well?"

"There was a woman on the board Ian. Not a person I expected to see here at this time. Have you any idea who she was supposed to be representing?"

"Don't tell me that this is equal rights for women in reverse? I did hear however that the person you are speaking of is very well qualified for that position even though she did not train in this country. But then one supposes that as we are all now European with freedom of movement between states that such an eventuality was inevitable. But tell me, why are you so uptight about the woman?"

"I am not uptight. It is simply that I have met her before and that meeting did little to convince me that she was the type of person one could expect to see sitting on the board!"

"Ah so you have met her before and because of that you imagined that you might curry some sort of favour?"

"That is total rubbish and certainly not worthy of you Ian. Still as we are to receive no news on her progress today I suggest we get out of this place and return to the office where at least Eric Taylor might be glad to see us!"

"You wouldn't be running away by any chance, would you?"

"Why not bury your adolescent type of humour for a change Ian. After all it is our duty to return and let Eric know how we both got on!"

"For myself I would be tempted to refuse for after all it is rather a special occasion today. But there again I doubt if Eric will be able to cope with the amount of tears you are likely to shed on his shoulder and therefore he will possibly need some sort of ally. Besides someone will be needed to tend to the shop whilst you unburden your fears on the boss!"

Rachel felt she could have hit him for such words of consolation but by that time Ian had moved out of her reach and all she could do was to dutifully follow him and make her way back again to the office.

"It was a piece of cake!" Eric had been waiting for their return to the office anxiously but upon the young man's words he frowned indicating that he felt none too pleased with this stripling's description of the board that they had attended.

"But then of course you were only taking the very first stage, a preliminary one might say in order to access whether you were worthy of continuing in the profession. In Rachel's case however the matter is slightly different!" No doubt Eric Taylor had been shrewd enough to recognise the dread in Rachel's eyes and was anxious to send the youngster packing before he endeavoured to speak to her.

"So what were your own impressions Rachel?" He had waited somewhat patiently as the young man showing disappointed that no one had hailed his prowess had departed from his room.

"Do I need to have any? If you want it in a nutshell Eric I am afraid that I failed my board and that is without any official confirmation of the fact!"

"So I take it that all did not go well? Can I ask in what respect?"

"There was a woman on the board. Someone I had not expected to see!"

"Ah then you must be speaking of Greta Silvo. I have not met the person but I have heard that the woman has excellent qualifications. Indeed she lectured in some University, not in this country on the very subject matter!"

"She has long finger nails!" The words had passed her lips before she realised what she had said.

"I take it that it was these then that distracted you from giving a complete résumé of your work?" Eric's tone now rang with some incredulity

"They must be false that is all that I can say!"

"Rachel this is not at all like you?"

"Greta Silvo happened to be on the cruise ship which I went on to play dog's body to Callum Rothwell. To my mind the woman did not appear to have a very nice nature. She was also acting as stenographer to one Pablo Capello, a diplomat of doubtful qualities. Indeed the pair of them made quite a frightening duo and not only, I would like to add, in the world of politics!"

"So am I to believe that this prior experience of the woman helped to sully your performance today?"

"I am not looking for excuses for my poor performance Eric, merely stating that I believe Pablo Capello to be guilty of flooring Callum on the quayside in Lisbon and as a result putting him into hospital. Neither can it be said that I received any good will from his stenographer on the homeward voyage!"

"For someone in your position Rachel these could be very damaging charges!"

"Maybe but nevertheless ones that I feel justified in making for their plots did not merely involve Callum but also one of the young Croatian diplomats whom they appeared determined to have arrested for murder!"

"Well I know that you have supposedly been studying Rachel but now I am beginning to wonder which books you have been studying from!"

For her part Rachel fell silent. It seemed almost impossible to reason with this man whom she had previously regarded as a friend. Not that she supposed that this was surprising for Eric Taylor had never been a man to view any aspects away from the straight and narrow path of his profession. She sensed his disappointment in her but under the circumstances felt that there was little she could have done about it and at least by unburdening her soul she had made some small attempt to put him into the picture. Not that on the surface at least she appeared to have made much impression.

"Then I suppose we will have to wait until the board release their findings on your enhancement!" His was his way now of issuing her a dismissal from his office. "In the meantime I am sure that you must have plenty to keep you occupied if only by making some attempt to catch up with the pile of work currently in your in-tray!"

"But of course!" Rachel gritted her teeth as she realised that their conversation had reached its conclusion. Yet although on the surface she did indeed try to apply herself to the tasks in hand Rachel was not a very happy bunny for so far she had found out little about Callum, not to mention having to attend upon the wishes of that she bitch who somehow now appeared to hold some sort of influence over the selection board. How this came to be she dreaded to think for now she must turn her mind onto matters far more mundane.

Nevertheless if Rachel had determined to put all thought of Greta to the back of her mind the same could not be said for her adversary. That evening Rachel determined to escape the office promptly and avoid running into any sneering comments that could possibly be passed by one certain young man, who after apparently feeling that he had done well at the board now wished to crow his advantage upon one he deemed had been a little less fortunate.

Leaving the building she was not immediately aware of that shadowy character waiting on the outside and even if she had noticed this creature she would never have deemed that this person had been waiting for her.

"Miss Burton, you will be pleased to come with me. There is a person who wishes to speak to you!"

At any other time Rachel would have walked past this specimen without a word but this time around she was soon aware that the man was holding a gun in her direction. "I have a car waiting to take us to our required destination!" He indicated the now open door to a limousine parked alongside of the pavement.

"In a nutshell I have no intention of going anywhere with you although perhaps you will tell me who it is who is so desperate to speak to me that they will apply such methods!" Perhaps her words sounded a great deal braver to how she felt herself at the time.

"I have no doubt that my mistress will be able to provide any such detail that you require. Now if it pleases you please get inside the vehicle!"

"Certainly not, I have no intention of doing any such thing!"

"My mistress did say that you had an awkward nature, therefore as you do not feel inclined to oblige I am afraid there is only one thing for it!"

Rachel had little recollection of how the blow was administered but the man was obviously used to getting his own way for the next thing she realised was that she was in the back of the vehicle that appeared to hurtle its way through the streets paying little attention to any passenger comfort!

If her mind had been filled with ideas of dwellings placed on the periphery of the city then once again her fears on that score were soon dispatched for the limousine finally pulled up outside a perfectly normal house on the outskirts of the city and once the vehicle had stopped Rachel was to find herself hustled out yet again and motioned at pistol point towards the door of the place.

"You will go inside?" Rachel wondered why the police had not been successful in removing gun crime from off the streets of the Metropolis. Yet now she had little option but to oblige. Perhaps though she was not totally surprised when after passing through those doors she found herself to be confronted by a figure that she immediately recognised, for Greta had certainly not bothered in pairing down those long finger nails. Yet she regarded the advent of the newcomer almost with a half-smile, almost indeed as if she was at one with what had transpired.

"I do hope that you will forgive the dramatics Rachel, I may call you that I presume?"

"That depends on exactly what you want for in truth I am unaccustomed to being subjected to such a hustle and transported to somewhere I had no particular reason for wanting to go!"

"But then naturally I presume you would like very much to hear how you went on with your board today!"

"Not particularly for I believe my performance resulted in quite a low rating!" Rachel pondered in her mind as to what the others motives could possibly be. Surely she had not been brought here merely for Greta to gloat over her abject performance?

"Of course that need not be necessarily true for a great deal can now depend on your co-operation in certain matters!" The girl drew herself up to her full height and for once abandoned the attention given to her nails.

"And what in particular are you talking about when you say co-operation?" Rachel wondered why she had bothered to ask the question for she knew instinctively that the answer would be readily provided without any requests on her behalf.

"The first question I wish to put to you is whether you have heard from Mr Rothwell recently?"

"The answer to that is quite simple. No, I have not, nor have I any idea as to the man's whereabouts so I will save you the opportunity from asking!" Rachel gritted her teeth. So this was what it was all about; an exchange of information in order to ensure that she would be successful in passing her board. The whole idea was completely alien to her and yet knowing this woman should she have expected anything better?

"Of course that is what I expected your answer to be for I know as well as you that the man has been spirited away, no doubt in an attempt to wreak more havoc on certain matters that I support. But that is of course not the only reason that you were invited here today and now I suppose you will be brimming over with curiosity to hear the second of my reasons!"

"Whatever that happens to be I cannot see that it has any bearing on my response!" So the woman was capable of vetoing her promotion prospects? Well so be it for even that was infinitely more preferable that paying some sort of homage in lieu of a debt of gratitude.

Nevertheless Greta still had yet another surprise awaiting her. Calling out to the back room she was rewarded with the appearance of a young man and the gasp that emitted from Rachel's lips at the sight of this person drew a callous smile across the lips of her abductor. "Of course I do not have to introduce you to your brother now do I?"

Rachel gazed mesmerised at the sight of the newcomer. The last thing she had heard of Steve was that he had gained a place in Oxford. How he had managed to do that had at the time been beyond her comprehension for Rachel had never credited Steve with having such academic qualifications.

"I suppose it wouldn't be asking too much of you to at least pretend that you are glad to see me?" The boy she had once considered to be a spoilt brat gazed at his sister as if commanding some response.

"I believed that you were currently at University?"

"I was until I flunked my course. Of course you know all about that don't you Rachel?"

"I hardly consider myself to be in the same position as what you are!"

"Ah but in my case I used my so called failure to secure an appointment in Paris. That in itself is something more meaningful than your own laid back existence working for some third rate accountant. For you see whilst I was in Paris I managed to rub shoulders with people at the University there. That of course is where I obtained my information from!"

"Sorry but you have lost me I am afraid. These people you met and obviously associated with? Who were they?"

"I did warn you Greta that Rachel here would attempt to play the big sister in wanting to vet my association of friends! Still it was not only in my meeting them that is significant but also the fact that they were quite able to acquaint me with a little history that until the present time has been confused with legend!"

"As usual you are once again talking in riddles Steve. One knew full well as a child that you could never bear to allow your feet to touch the ground!"

"Perhaps it would be to your advantage to hear your brother out!" She wondered whether it was her imagination or whether Greta actually was growing in impatience to get to the end of this saga. "Therefore perhaps you ought to let this child finish off what he is about to tell you!"

Steve seemed undeterred with Greta's interjection for come what may he was still determined to finish off his story. "There are some very interesting and yet quite unexplained riddles within French history: Matters that in the past have been recorded before being brushed to one side. Yet in the present climate with the Euro faltering in its present state, investors are looking in the direction of certain commodities that are not noted for losing value in the long term. Our saga indeed dates back to stories of the Spanish Main where marauding privateers also patrolled the seaways with one eye open for opportunity!"

"No doubt your recital possesses a vivid and creative story line Steve but as yet I fail to see how this involves me?"

"Have you heard of the Cape Verde Islands?"

"Should I have heard?"

"Only in so far as one of more notable admirals Sir Francis Drake had dealings with the place on at least two occasions. The first time he went there it was in order to plunder and yet he was to return to leave cannon for their protection. Something that appeared to be a rather bizarre action unless one considers that maybe he considered a good enough place to unload some of the spoils he had no wish to declare. Now with the present economic climate our friends in Europe are anxious to discover if such rumours from the past are true!"

"I have still no idea how your imaginative notions have anything to do with me?"

"Not so much you Rachel but perhaps something to do with the company you have been keeping. That is why we would like to know the present whereabouts of your friend Callum Rothwell for at such a crucial moment we do not appreciate his involvement with the Eurozone nor his attitude upon such matters!"

"I thought that I had already made it perfectly clear that I have no idea where Callum currently is. Neither do I consider any such strategy as he has is anything to do with me!"

"And if the outcome was related to your own recent experience when you were interviewed by the board, would that not have some bearing on the case?" Again Greta had drawn herself into the sort of position of an animal ready to charge although perhaps thinking the better of this movement she turned her attention back again onto her nails.

"I'm afraid that even if I did want to help you in this matter which is something I am not totally convinced that I do, I still am unable to help!"

"That I consider is a great pity because I am afraid that unless you have a change of heart you will have to remain here as our guest. After all we would hardly appreciate you opening your lips in the wrong place and perhaps inadvertently revealing our intentions to an outsider!"

"Now you really must be joking. I think that I have heard just about enough. I cannot help you by telling you Callum's current whereabouts and no doubt if he heard the fictitious nonsense you have just told me it would afford him a good laugh!" Whether her brother was present or not, Rachel made her way towards the door. There however she found that her exit had been barred by two burly individuals who most definitely had been instructed not to let her pass!

★ ★ ★ ★

Chapter Seven

Ian Calvert took a long sip from the pint that lay on the table in front of him. To be fair the man ought to have been elated by this time for he had just obtained the news that he had passed his board and was therefore ready to proceed onto the next rung of the ladder in his chosen career. Yet Ian Calvert found that at the moment such a mood escaped him for although in one sense he was overjoyed at having succeeded in passing his board, the fact that he had been unable to crow about his success to Rachel Burton had possibly rubbed a little of the glitter of his achievement away. For there had been no sign at the office of Rachel that day, much to Eric Taylor's annoyance, a factor that had in turn reflected on his own success, for few had taken notice of his own achievement with Rachel apparently being missing. Nor could it be said that there had been any message from this girl explaining her absence and even Ian could not believe that this was simply due to sour grapes, just because she herself had not done as well as she had expected, for whilst the two of them often sparred within the office precincts Ian still held the woman in high regard even if he kept such matters close to his chest.

To add to his perplexion there had also been another person in that bar earlier on that same evening. A young man he had recognised vaguely for Ian remembered that this person had been a freshman at the University at the same time as himself but then, after what had appeared to be a short space of time, this undergraduate had disappeared. Rumours had circulated he remembered that the other person had changed his allegiance to Paris but whether that had been by design or because of a factor that had been enforced upon him for some reason Ian had never found out. Not at that stage in his career he had been particularly interested. Indeed the character had almost faded from his mind until tonight when for some apparent reason the fellow had himself been in the bar earlier on and much to Ian's surprise he had claimed recognition of him.

Maybe one reason why this meeting had remained in his memory was the fact that the stranger had upon first sight, looked unduly pleased with himself and therefore Ian had little doubt that the fellow was seeking someone now to whom he could brag of some achievement.

"I am not mistaken am I? It is Ian Calvert isn't it? I guess I haven't seen you for absolutely ages, indeed not since we were freshmen together!" Perhaps Ian should have been aware even at this stage that the other had something to brag about, something that the man considered could possibly light the flames of envy in Ian's eyes. "Do tell me how you are getting on. Indeed what are you doing with yourself nowadays. Of course I presume that you eventually qualified?"

"I did yes and I am now working locally with a firm of accountants!"

"How positively boring that sounds!" The other wrinkled up his nose in an attitude of disgust.

"What of you yourself?" Ian knew full well that the other was now waiting for this question and after uttering the words that would invite some sort of explanation he almost regretted having done so.

"My expectations certainly exceed a parochial level. But then of course I had the opportunity to be able to study into matters that could yet yield me a personal fortune!"

"You make it sound intriguing at least!" Ian had decided that such a trivial conversation could help to allay the feeling of injustice he still believed that he had committed in Rachel's direction earlier on.

"You mean that I will be able to make my fortune whilst you still remain an office boy? Yes I suppose that you can consider that it is. But then of course I had the opportunity to study something of the exploits of our medieval ancestors, of privateers and their quest for gold bullion, which did not always go to the people who had commissioned them in the first place. Treasure that until this day remains largely undiscovered by modern man. Although one must admit that in the present economic climate there are still those who are willing to finance such expeditions in an attempt to trace such a reward. After all our financiers would appreciate being able to lay their hands on gold bullion in the present climes, would you not agree, for gold is after all a commodity that retains its value even if it does not increase in its worth?"

To be honest Ian was now becoming slightly bored with the other man's pontificating and yet the newcomer's next phase served to have him pondering as to what was coming next.

"I believe that you are employed by Eric Taylor?"

"Yes as a matter of fact I am!"

"In that case perhaps you will inform him that my sister will not be returning to the fold; not that is until she sees fit to help us with some enquiries which we consider to be of some importance to our cause!"

"Rachel Burton is your sister?" Ian allowed the tenet of curiosity to now echo in his voice.

"But of course although I must admit that before today I had not seen her for some considerable time. Still there appears to be one or two items that we now have to straighten out with her, for my superiors are quite convinced that allowing so many immigrants into the country from other parts of the E.U is taking employment away from our own workforce. Secondly I have been also been informed that it is also imperative for Britain to support the rest of the E.U on its monetary policies!"

"So you are now suggesting that your sister is stopping the country from doing this? Forgive me but I find that hard to believe"

"Rachel has contacts who are definitely trying to move matters in that direction. Now at this time we would like to know the exact whereabouts of one of these people so that he might be persuaded into rethinking his policies!"

"Forgive me if I have got this wrong but are you saying that you are holding Rachel about this matter?"

"Not me personally although I can assure you that she will be well looked after and she will be able to return to your dreary little office work just as soon as she complies with our request!"

"Then if you purport to be her brother I can hardly visualise any family affection if this is the way you are carrying on!"

"The result of our endeavours is important for a great many people, many of whom have invested a great deal of capital in the outcome. In the meantime you need have no fear that any harm will befall her for I have Greta's word on that. Therefore perhaps you will be kind enough to pass on the details regarding Rachel's absence to your employer for after all I would hate the girl to lose her job, however mediocre that appears to be!"

Perhaps Ian was too flabbergasted to make a response for instead when the man left the young man picked up his beer glass and asked for a refill. Surely he had a great deal to attempt to digest and indeed believe if what he had just been told was actually true, for he still had it in mind that this must be some sort of a spoof.

He was still in this frame of mind, toying with his conscience, and at a loss to know whether Rachel had been kidnapped or not and whether he should indeed report the matter, for after all the man imparting the message had been Rachel's own brother and surely such blood ties would bear well for her, when a further person entered the bar. Ian had met Brett Chaplain once before when he had lectured at his University but nevertheless did not think that this man would recognise him when at the time he had been but a lowly student.

In this assumption however Ian was quite wrong although it was not so much as Brett remembering him from his more youthful days but rather that the other man realised that Ian worked for Eric Taylor.

"I believe I am right in assuming that you work for an associate of mine, a person who goes under the name of Eric Taylor?" Ian found himself gazing up into a pair of vivid blue eyes and under the circumstances could do little else but nod. "I believe that I am also right in stating that Rachel Burton is also a colleague of yours. Have you any idea of where I can find her? Apparently she never returned home from work today and it now appears that it is imperative that I see her!"

"The lady suddenly appears to be in big demand!"

"And what precisely do you mean by that?"

"Simply that her brother has just left the bar area where you are currently standing after telling me a yarn that I hardly find feasible. Oh I admit she did not do too well with her board earlier on but what has transpired since that time seems to be more than a little far-fetched!"

"Perhaps you would care to enlighten me?" The man had sat down opposite to him and did not appear to be for moving until Ian provided some of the detail. In his present state of mind Ian was only too eager to oblige if only to relieve some of the inner tension he was currently suffering, whereupon he saw the other grip his knuckles tightly!"

"Tell me have I heard you correctly? You said the girl in question was currently in the company of one Greta Silvio?"

"The name of Greta was mentioned yes. Apparently it is felt that Rachel holds the key to some mystery or other which these people desperately want to find out about. I was merely told to inform the boss that she wouldn't be returning to work in the near future although the one who called himself her brother gave me some ear ache with the amount of garbage he enunciated. All I can say is that if that was Rachel's brother I am glad I don't have to meet the rest of the family!"

"I believe Rachel has previously termed her brother as being a damned nuisance!" A half smile caught at Brett's lips but this was quickly removed as a more serious vogue overcame him. "You were positive however that Rachel is now being entertained by one Greta Silvio?"

"That was what the man said. Look Rachel and I have had our differences on the work front but I don't want to land her in any more trouble. What am I supposed to tell our employer if she doesn't turn up in the morning?"

"Perhaps you can consider that the matter is now well in hand for Eric Taylor already knows what Rachel has recently been involved in and if I am now successful in my endeavours then I will inform the man myself!"

"Exactly what do you mean by your endeavours?" Curiosity had now apparently replaced the feeling of apprehension that Ian had initially felt.

"Shall we say that I am acquainted with Greta Silvio and I have a fair idea as to where I will currently be able to find the female?"

The boy's eyes opened wide for now he felt that he was definitely missing out on something and the thought of missing out was something that Ian did not fully appreciate, but by this time Brett had stood obviously anxious to continue with his quest and this motion was not something that included the other. "You will of course say nothing to Eric Taylor about this matter until after I have phoned the man for myself!" The words were spoken almost like a command and Ian, much to his own disapproval, found himself nodding in agreement. Brett left with a nod and a brief smile and suddenly the bar area seemed to be a much quieter place. The boy was left to reflect that maybe he should not have behaved in such a manner previously towards Rachel but then at that time he had no idea that she was somehow involved with all these intricacies. Solemnly he finished the pint that lay in front of him before leaving the pub, his idea of having some sort of celebration for doing well at his board now having completely disappeared from out of his mind!.

Brett knew exactly where Greta Silvio was currently staying in that city simply because he had made it his business to find out earlier that day and therefore hiring a taxi it did not take him long to arrive at the rented accommodation. His only concern was the possibility that Pablo Capello would also be there and for good measure Brett touched an object currently in his pocket as if for some form of reassurance.

Still if the woman in question was surprised to see him when he knocked on the door of this property she did not at first reveal this for instead she greeted the man with the same gushing overtones as she had employed on previous occasions and Brett allowed himself to savour a moment of relief for this must surely mean that Capello was not there at the present time.

"Indeed this is a surprise Brett, but I must say a pleasant one. But tell me what are you doing here?" The woman was by this time rapidly smoothing her hair and cursing herself that possibly she had not found the opportunity to look her best.

"I guess that unfortunately this is not a social visit Greta so you can spare yourself the effort of applying the glamour for my sake. I am merely here to collect one Rachel Burton whom I presume you appear to be entertaining at the moment, so to these ends can I suggest that you call your hit men off for the night!"

"And why do you presume that Rachel Burton is here?" The other woman stood obstinately in his path.

"Because quite frankly I was more than a little surprised when you chose to seek to confide in children, especially those still living with the ideals of youth and who apparently have not yet learnt that art of keeping their own counsel!"

"Then I presume you have been speaking to Steve Burton the girl's brother?"

"The idealist, no, more is the pity for I guess I would like to have met this young person whom his sister described as something of a damned nuisance. Instead I was informed of matters by one of his contemporaries who quite fortunately does not appear to hold the same extremist views on the subject matter as Steve himself!"

"The boy spoke a great deal of nonsense I admit!"

"But not total nonsense when he touched on the matter of investors seeking to protect their financial interests in this present clime by obtaining gold. Investors I would suggest, who were a little like your own associate Pablo Capello in their mistaken beliefs!" Brett witnessed the girl start and realised that perhaps his words were not too far away from the truth.

"I know nothing of gold, merely the fact that we require to know the present whereabouts of Callum Rothwell, something that I believe the girl already knows!"

"And what if she doesn't know: Have you considered that Greta?"

"But of course she must have some idea. The two of them were close is that not a fact?"

This time it was Brett's turn to wince on those words an action that delighted the beleaguered Greta as she found such indications that the two had been close were having the required reaction on her caller

"Whether indeed that was a fact or otherwise does not alter the situation for I believe I am right in saying that Rachel Burton is currently here with you and not exactly here of her own free will!" Whatever Brett's feelings were on the matter of Rachel and Callum's association he had mastered the art of being able to disguise the matter.

"But I thought that we were friends Brett? In which case perhaps I might have expected more support from you!" Perhaps Greta considered that by pouting she might possibly achieve her objective but by this time Brett had unceremoniously pushed past her and entered the house.

"Leaving any friendship you claim we have on one side I would like to make it quite clear that I have no intention of leaving this place without the girl!"

Greta glanced at his face. Perhaps she was surprised to see the stubborn look that now passed across his features. Nevertheless the woman was still of the opinion that she held the whip hand and after pressing a bell on the hall table she was indeed rewarded with the appearance of one of her minders. "Sorry Brett but I am afraid that I am unable to do business with you!"

Brett glanced at the individual who was even then advancing in his direction, so it appeared that Greta must have a contingent of such burly individuals that she was rather fond of using in order to get her own way. "Then I consider it to be a great pity that our relationship should end in this manner!" The newcomer may have appeared to be tough but even so the man baulked at the sight of the gun which Brett had suddenly produced. "If you know what is good for you bring the girl in here!"

The other man hesitated but only for a moment especially when he saw Brett's fingers move towards the trigger. It was the second person who finally brought Rachel into the room, again a brute well used to using his fists but not a lethal weapon and glancing at his companion he pushed the tear stained and obviously distressed girl in Brett's direction.

"Pablo will not like this I warn you!" At least Greta attempted to make some sound of protest.

"To be frank with you Greta I don't give a damn what Pablo likes and what he doesn't like. After all I have had to put up with enough of his idiosyncrasies' of late! Perhaps it might be as well Rachel if you made a move towards the front door whilst I continue to torment these tough guys with this toy!"

In truth Rachel did not think to raise any objection. The girl was still obviously confused and disorientated after what had happened but the promise of fresh air in her lungs appeared to be enough to make her act.

"Now get in that taxi!" Perhaps it was more than fortunate that one was standing by but then Brett had previously told the man to wait and although the driver was obviously taken aback with what was happening he had been previously paid a retaining fee. Following her but still holding the weapon as a threat to those who attempted to stop them Brett almost barked the order at her and Rachel obeyed almost as if she was automated.

"We will bid you a fond farewell!" It was almost a tongue in cheek remark as once he had established that Rachel had done as she was told Brett followed, instructing the driver to rev up the car in order for then to get away from the place as quickly as possible.

"Are you all right?" They had driven away from the scene before Brett, realising the girl was still shaking, glanced in her direction and Rachel still not knowing properly what was happening but only glad to be away from that place of confinement attempted to nod her response. "Good!" He lent across to give the driver some instructions. "In that case we will stop at your apartment long enough for you to pick up your passport. I presume that you have the document handy?"

"Yes but -----what do I need my passport for anyway? It's not that I am not grateful but --!"

"We are flying to Brussels tonight. You can tell me about your itinerant brother on the way!"

"But --------!"

"No buts please! For once in your life you will do as you are told without argument!"

"But I will need a case------!"

"If you think we have time for you to stop and start packing up then you can think again. Time my dear girl is now of the essence!"

Rachel glanced in his direction as the car finally stopped outside of her apartment. Now feeling somewhat mesmerised by what this individual had been saying she had almost forgotten her previous encounter.

But her stillness was not enough to satisfy her companion.

"Now go girl and get your wretched documentation. I thought that I had made myself clear, time is of the essence!" Nor was Brett content to allow her to move in her own time for getting out of the car himself he then moved to open the door at her side and before standing like some task master over her whilst she complied with his command and when she had retrieved the documentation he then summoned the by now confused taxi proprietor to drive like a man obsessed in the direction of the airport.

Indeed it was only after the two of them had cleared immigration and custom control that he finally paused to look at her.

"Now go and rinse your face so folk won't think that I am abducting you!" He motioned her away from the magazine stall in the direction of the ladies. "Don't even think of buying any magazine for you have no time to read on board. Your time will be spent in giving me an explanation into your brother's exploits!"

Perhaps Rachel considered she was acting like a zombie in obliging him. But at the time her mind refused to focus on anything but the commanding note he held in his voice and after taking a look at herself in the mirror in the place she decided that he was probably right for the tears that had filtered from her eyes earlier on that night had done nothing to enhance her looks.

"Well is that any better?" She did not keep the man waiting for long after swilling her face. Perhaps she secretly felt that he might have ventured into the place in search of her but on the other hand she also remembered that he had mentioned Brussels and that was where Eric Taylor had previously intimated to her that this was the place where Callum now was.

"Time to go to the gate, we have already been called!" He did not reply to her question but simply motioned her in the direction of the required boarding gate. In fact Brett did not say another word until they were safely installed on the plane although Rachel herself now had repercussions wondering how on earth he had managed to get through the airport carrying that weapon that he had brandished earlier. In fact it was finally Rachel, unable to contain her thoughts any longer, who was the one to finally open the conversation.

"You had a gun?" She had the vision of Brett's lips twitching before he let out a laugh.

"And you assumed that I had no more sense than to try and bring it through an airport? Any way you can rest assured that it was Government Issue; for carrying a weapon is not usually my style and in any event it was not so much a gun as a Taser. Still be thankful that I didn't have to use it for I am sure that I would have missed the target, in which case we both could have been in trouble. But we are not here to talk about my prowess with weaponry but rather about your brother and how you managed to finish up in that predicament?"

"Why are we going to Brussels?" She wondered whether she was actually avoiding speaking about Steve for in all fairness she did not want to especially after what had happened so recently when he had turned up at

Greta's only to talk verbal rubbish about some mythical Islands.

"We are going to Brussels yes. But the reason why we are going there will have to wait until you answer the question I put to you first!"

"I thought that I had already made it clear that I consider my brother to be nothing more than a damned nuisance. Considered to be clever at school he managed to win himself a place at Oxford only to transfer after a very short time to some University in France, much to my parents' disgust at the time. I think that was when they decided to go to the States for a time simply to get out of the way. Anyway whilst he was there he apparently became attracted to some characters that apparently were as peculiar as what he was himself and who also had some rather obnoxious ideas about our present society. That was the last I heard of him!"

"Until tonight I believe! What exactly happened tonight and how did you finish up at Greta's?"

"Today or was it yesterday, I am afraid I can't remember now but I took my board and fared rather badly I am afraid. I am not making excuses but I think my apparent failure was due in no small part to the fact that Greta Silvio happened to be on the board, although why she should be in that position I have no idea. Anyway after work there was a car waiting for me and although I did not go with these people willingly I was told that Greta wanted to see me and believing that perhaps this had something to do with her being on the board that had judged my performance, I presumed, quite wrongly of course that I might learn something to my advantage. The only thing that I learnt was that my brother was also present at this address, whereupon I was treated to a discourse of utter rubbish. One thing that I did discover however was that the only thing these people wished to learn from me was the whereabouts of Callum Rothwell and despite my protests that I did not know I was told that I would stay there until I was willing to reveal the truth!"

"Yet I believe that you did know where Callum now is?"

"If I did do you really think I would have told the people I believe to be responsible for his accident?"

"And who exactly do you believe caused this so called accident then?"

"I happened to see Pablo Capello whilst I was in London with Adri. He still bears the mark on his cheek that I believe the girl on the boat gave to him before he killed her. Why he killed her I do not know apart from the fact that he wanted to disgrace Adri who later turned out to be a member of the Croatian delegation. Pablo was seen in an argument with Callum on the quayside in Lisbon and therefore if he committed one crime then why not a second, especially when he had his aide de camp in Greta to support him?" She saw Brett nod in agreement and then as if to change the subject altogether.

"Have you fastened your seat belt?"

"Of course I have, what do you take me for? But now I have told you my story you did promise to tell me why we are going to Brussels?"

"We are going there simply for your own safety Rachel. After considering what was now transpiring in the U.K. it was decided in your own interests that you should be moved somewhere to a place of safety where we could endeavour to keep an eye on you!"

"Touching one could concede!" She noted that he had never mentioned Callum in his explanation. "That is of course always supposing that I am willing to go!"

"Under the circumstances you now appear to have little option!"

"In that case perhaps you can explain how you managed to find me and how indeed you found out about my brother?"

"Your release was made possible by the information we received from one of your junior colleagues. At the time the man appeared to be having a bad day. Whether that was because he had a guilt complex at doing well at his board as opposed to you, is a matter of conjecture. But then it also appeared that your brother could not stop bragging about his own fortunes when the two of them met in the pub, a matter that your colleague took exception to!"

"You are saying that it was Ian who informed you of my whereabouts?"

"The boy did his best although he was still overwhelmed with what his ex-college intern had just told him and it so happened that I came on the scene only a short time after this had transpired!"

"But how did you know Ian?" Now Rachel was determined to ferret out the truth from this man although her question was once again greeted with a rather passive smile almost indeed as if Brett was questioning why her focus remained on what he considered to be trivia.

"As a matter of fact I did remember him from his student days although to be fair I also knew that the man worked alongside of your good self at your noted establishment. But there is far more to the synopsis than a casual meeting. We have been aware for some time that in the present economic climate, more especially with the down grading of the credit rating in several Eurozone countries, not to mention the unstable element behind the Euro itself, that many of our more wealthy financiers had been seeking other means of investment rather than abiding by the Eurozone economy with the threat of eventually losing some if not all of their assets. Thus investing in gold bullion rather than in the Euro appealed to their monetary senses and your brother, for his own reasons was unwittingly able to shed some light onto this matter for us!"

"But I am afraid that I still fail to understand how this affects me and why I now appear to be being hustled into the hubbub of the financial centre in Brussels!"

"Again you appear to have got hold of the wrong end of the stick. As I previously explained you are being moved out of circulation for your own protection and nothing else. But as a point of interest I believe that you were quite wrong in assuming that it was Pablo who was the one who dealt Callum the blow that floored him. Not that I assume he was completely innocent of the incident. But if he had been the one who delivered the punch then doubtless such an action would have been observed from off the decks of the ship at the time when it happened for it is true to say that many of these travellers have an inbuilt sense that it is their ritual to observe when a boat is casting off from any port and the fact that the ship delayed its departure because of one passenger who had not reported back would no doubt have whetted their enthusiasm. Yet as far as I am aware no one reported seeing anything of such an incident. Therefore I am of the opinion that Pablo must have persuaded Callum to follow him somewhere and it was in this place where the innocent lamb actually ventured that Callum received the blow that rendered him unconscious!"

"Look who exactly are you Brett?" Her discomfort now pushed to the back of her mind Rachel began to exhibit some elements of curiosity.

"But I thought that I had already told you once in the distant past. I am footloose and fancy free and intend to enjoy the good things in life!"

"You also appear to be eloquent in your fabrications of the truth. Can I take it then that you are now taking me to see Callum?"

"If you are asking whether that is my prior motivation for taking you to Brussels then I am afraid that the answer is no!"

"Then might I be permitted to question why you are not? I believe you said that I was being taken there for my own safety?"

"So I did. On the other hand my department does not exactly co-habit the same one that Callum is assigned to, for our friend is more concerned with foreign policy especially when this affects the Eurozone!"

"Then what exactly are your own concerns? I presume from what you are saying that you are trying to tell me that Callum knows nothing of my potential arrival in Brussels?"

"That is correct at this moment in time for my own brief happens to hold finances as its prime motivating force and from what I have learnt from both you and your brother the task of stabilising the Euro will be made all the more difficult if our investors are persuaded to switch their finances elsewhere. What you may not yet be aware of is that several countries within the Eurozone have recently been downgraded losing their three star plus rating. And that factor is causing some concern amongst my colleagues. Therefore it is a possibility that your own information will now be of some use to them?"

"And might I be permitted to ask who these people are whom you hold such respect for?"

"If it will put an end to your never ceasing barrage of questions I will tell you. I suppose that even you must have heard of the International Monetary Fund?"

Rachel gulped. Of course she had heard of them but on the other hand the very mention of this illustrious bunch stilled her into a silence as she tried to piece together what had happened in her mind but she failed dismally in her attempt. At least Brett now appeared pleased with her silence for he even went as far as to retrieve a notebook from his pocket for as far as he was concerned their present conversation was now at an end.

It was not a very long flight to Brussels, certainly not long enough for Rachel to rationalise what had happened in her mind for it only seemed to be seconds later when her companion dutifully informed her that they were approaching the landing. Still there was one thing that she was sure about and that was if she was in Brussels then she would make every effort to seek out Callum if only to seek his reaction to what was currently happening.

"There will be a car waiting for us when we have cleared the formalities!" Brett now spoke in a matter of fact voice, a factor that reminded her of someone else.

"As I now appear to have been abducted for whatever reason from my own country perhaps in all fairness I should be allowed to contact my employer. After all the man has shown that he has the patience of a saint in putting up with me of late and therefore I feel that he deserves some sort of explanation as to my absence!"

"That of course will not be necessary. If you are speaking of Eric Taylor then I believe the man has already been informed. Not I grant you that the man is not suffering from some sort of confusion on the issue but then as an ex college lecturer himself he probably understands far more than what you are willing to give him credit for. And now if you are ready we will attempt our passage through immigration and with a little bit of luck they will believe that we are a couple and therefore they will not be too stringent over our arrival!"

Still feeling a little mesmerised Rachel made to follow him from the plane into the airport terminal. Just as he had previously said there was a car waiting outside for them the driver tapping on the dashboard anxiously until he saw them make an appearance and Rachel almost without thought found herself cloistered inside. The memory of that previous car that had been waiting to whisk her away to Greta's was now even more deeply entrenched in her mind and she wondered why she had put so much trust in Brett quite so willing when previously she had possessed suspicions about him.

"So old habits die hard?" He had obviously judged her mood and possibly the ideas that were currently invading her mind. "Well I can assure you that you are not being abducted this time around we just require your help that is all and after that you are a free agent!"

"You said that and yet I noted that you kept my passport?"

"But of course. I have already told you that you were brought here for your own safety amongst other things. And I can hardly conscribe that the idea of you trying to return to the U.K without our knowledge would be in line with that ideal!"

Unable to muster a response Rachel turned her head away glancing through the car window as the streets appeared to pass them by with monotonous regularity. Finally when she had just about given up any hope of ever reaching a destination, the vehicle stopped and

Rachel found herself gazing up at a newly constructed apartment block, its stone walls gleaming as the source of those floodlights served to illuminate it.

"Guess this is it!" Brett motioned her out of the vehicle and moving across to the reception area spoke quickly to the night porter in charge who immediately handed over some keys. "And now perhaps we will acquaint you with your accommodation!" He motioned the still mesmerised girl in the direction of the lift.

"But I can't stay here, I have no case remember!" He looked almost piteously in her direction as she let out a single wail. "You wouldn't let me stop to collect my case remember?"

"I believe you will find a robe and toiletries that will suffice for tonight" Applying the key he swung open the door and motioned her inside. "At least without clothes I will know where to find you in the morning, and there is also a breakfast tray and brewing facilities in the kitchen area for you to use. I will be around by ten thirty to supply you with your programme for the day. Until then I would advise you to try and get some rest. You are perfectly safe here so there is nothing for you to worry about!"

She had barely stepped inside the place when she heard the door click and realised that he had gone. Wandering around the place she soon realised that it contained all the facilities she would require yet her mind was still far too befuddled to take all this on board, for she was still wrestling with the question as to why she had been brought here. Brett had been eager to state that it was for her own safety but even if this was the case and he spoke the truth then it certainly appeared that he had succeeded in bringing her quite a long way from her local habitat.

Finally entering the bathroom with all of its deluxe appendages however seemed to break the continuum of her thoughts for the promise of a long relaxing soak in the large bath that lay before her proved to be only too tempting and she promised herself that she would soak her weary frame whilst continuing with her ponderous state. Perhaps indeed it was the very warmth of that water that helped to lull and dissipate such thoughts into the background of her mind and immersing her body in that soothing environment it was consequently much later when she finally emerged from that environ to don the robe that was apparently intended to serve as her sleeping apparel.

It would have been so easy for her to now sink away to peaceful slumbers in that inviting bed but almost by ritual she switched on the television set in her room in time to catch the late news. Most of the headlines dwelt on the cruise ship that had recently run aground and the rescue efforts currently under way even in the darkness of the night. The thought of this happening caused a shiver to run through her frame as she remembered that she too had recently been on one of those ships and although much had happened during that voyage it certainly could not compare with the current trauma that these passengers were currently undergoing.

Thinking of their obvious predicament almost made her miss the following news item which stated that the British Chancellor had not over ruled the idea of forwarding more money to support the I.M.F. if the crisis in the Eurozone deteriorated at the rate anticipated by many of the economists and now her mind circulated on the fact that Brett had stated that he had something to do with that organisation. Moreover Brett had appeared to be on more than friendly terms with Greta and more particular her aide de camp Pablo. This of course was a factor that she knew from the meetings that she had attended with Callum when they had appeared anxious to win the right to obtain more money from Britain. Now a firm resolution gelled in her mind, she had to find Callum and find out exactly what was going on. From all accounts this man was in Brussels and so was she now as a matter of fact.

Yet musing over these matters she had underestimated her lack of sleep or the sleep potion supplied by using that hot tub. And therefore Rachel was no longer able to do any thinking for the tenets of sleep had already attacked her senses and shortly afterwards unable to resist this onslaught that attacked her senses Rachel was fast asleep!

★ ★ ★ ★

Chapter Eight

Once Rachel had drifted away from her initial restless state she must indeed have slept solidly for the next thing she remembered was that insistent tapping on her room door and finally opening her eyes she could already see that the strands of daylight were percolating through the blinds in her room.

"Who is it?" Sleepily she searched for her slippers under the bed only to remember a few moments later that she had none. Indeed the only night attire she possessed was the robe that she now pulled more closely around her.

"It is the housekeeper Madam. I have a parcel here that has just been delivered for you!"

Perhaps one could have considered her a little unwise to have answered the call so eagerly for after all she had no knowledge of this person but upon just waking such thoughts did not immediately occur to Rachel. Indeed the girl was still in the throes of trying to puzzle out where on earth she was. In any event upon opening the door she discovered that the person currently standing there was exactly who she had portrayed herself to be, the housekeeper.

"The gentleman, the one who brought you here last night asked me to give you this parcel!" Upon these words the maid thrust the large box into Rachel's hands. "He said that you would need the items for later this morning and he judged them to be the right size!" With the last phrase the woman frowned as if she did not consider man to be any judge in such matters. "He said to remember that he will be around by ten thirty to pick you up!" And with that the woman sniffed as if she had related this message against her better judgement but now having done so was anxious to depart.

"What time is it now?" For the life of her Rachel could not remember where she had placed her watch.

"Why, it has just turned nine thirty. Don't tell me that you forgot to put your watch on. But then looking at you I suspect you will have to get cracking. You'll find a continental breakfast alongside of your tea tray. I guess that will be enough to put you on whilst you get yourself ready!" And with this the woman decided that she had completed her duty and made to leave for there were plenty of other matters she had to attend to besides pandering to one English girl whom she considered to have been rather foolhardy to have travelled to Brussels without any luggage.

Rachel glanced at the box the woman had thrust into her arms and decided that there was only one thing she could do and that was to open it. Inside the first thing she noticed however was a note.

"Sorry but I have just realised that I made you leave the U.K. in rather a hurry without having time to collect a case. I'm afraid that I had to guess at your size in order to equip you with something more suitable for you to wear today so I only hope it fits all right!"

With something of a start Rachel glanced down at the contents of the box. Neatly folded in its wrappings was a navy tailor made suit complete with a white blouse to wear underneath, tights that were destined to fit a variety of sizes and a pair of heeled sandals with a further note attached that he considered such footwear would be adaptable to her size of foot. Glancing at the clothes she had travelled in before discarding them, much against her will, she decided that the suit was probably the more suitable apparel to wear and after a quick wash found that the judgement in size was not bad at all. In fact it made her wonder if Brett made a habit of bestowing such niceties on his guests. The sandals however were a little more difficult, at least she felt sure she could have done with a bigger size, but if these were what she had to cram her feet into instead of the rather worn flats she had travelled to this place in, then so be it.

She attempted to cram a little of the pre-packed breakfast into her but found that she didn't really feel hungry. Thirsty yes and the teas she brewed helped to soothe a throat that was already feeling parched. Then she took a look at herself in the bathroom mirror before searching her handbag in desperation to find a comb. Not that she was fortunate to find any make up in there to take the shine off her face but then the man could not expect everything especially after the way she had been hustled here to this place.

In truth she was not ready a moment too soon for promptly at ten thirty her escort arrived and by this time she had woken up sufficiently well to allow a tenet of curiosity as to what all this was about to steal over her. Consequently upon his arrival she promptly left the room to venture downstairs into the Metropolis of Brussels.

His glance upon greeting her was one of approval, not she suspected so much on herself but rather on the fact that he appeared to have succeeded with his purchase. “So I managed to guess your size right. The colour suits you by the way. At least you look more presentable to meet the board in that!”

“The shoes are a little tight!” She determined that he was not going to have things all his own way.

“That was why I got the sandals. I wasn’t sure of your size but I thought sandals more adaptable!”

“With heels this height I probably won’t be able to walk. Neither do I happen to possess any make up with me!” She felt born to argue her cause.

“As far as the heels are concerned you haven’t got far to walk because I have the car with me. As far as your make up is concerned that matter can be rectified later. As it is I believe the board will be more likely to believe someone with a fresh morning face than a person with makeup splattered across it! Now are you going to get into the car for we are due to meet the board at eleven and that is a body who so happen who do not appreciate being kept waiting!"

The mention of meeting a board made Rachel shrink for the memory of that other board and her consequent failure was still fresh in her mind. "Then perhaps you will be good enough to explain what board you are speaking of and why on earth they should want to see me!" She held onto the car door as she spoke unwilling to go further until she got some sort of satisfactory response from him.

"Perhaps you are now forgetting where you are. This is Brussels and as such it so happens to house the headquarters of the Eurozone representatives. The people who have requested your presence here today happen to be members of the I.M.F as I am myself for it is felt that you have got some interesting information to share with us!"

"And what is that supposed to mean?" Rachel still stubbornly held onto that door unwilling to admit her surprise at learning that Brett was a member of the I.M.F and she wondered that if this was the case why he had not admitted to the fact sooner.

"Please will you get into this car? I have already said that you have a wealth of information to share with us, perhaps starting off with your own brother and his weird concoctions of where the Eurozone financiers are looking to invest their wealth in the current economic climate. For someone with a degree in economics you must have heard of that!"

"I know nothing about my brothers manoeuvres if that is what you are implying!" Perhaps inadvertently or even because she was now determined to make the point, by this time she had got into the vehicle and Brett had started the engine.

"Whether that is true or not you heard the man's story however fabricated that was at first hand, which puts you in a good position to relate what he said! I also believe that there are other things they want to ask you about!"

She fell silent during the rest of the journey which did not take long as she pondered on what Brett had said. Something, she determined did not sound to be exactly right to her ears. Still Rachel's first impression upon reaching these headquarters was of the ridiculous opulence that they seemed to be surrounded by in a city where some of the Euros used for that project could have been employed instead on improving other features. "We will park here!" Brett had pulled into a car parking space hallmarked for members of that illustrious body. "We have not far to walk across the terrazzo so just be careful you don't slip with those heels you are wearing on the marble floor!"

Whilst her determination to walk in those heels could be said to be admirable Rachel felt sure she could sense then gleam of laughter in her companions eyes as she made her attempt to cross that terrazzo and she cursed the fact that in truth she was unaccustomed to walking in objects with heels so high, for she could hardly term them as shoes, yet fortunately she did not slip for to have done so would have only succeeded in bringing forth a feeling of humiliation at such a plight. Besides by this time she was convinced that such white marble walls that lay in front of her contained the eyes of these so called European diplomats who had so little to do that watching a girl slip in her folly would have served to provide some entertainment for them. As she mounted the steps at the end of this parade ground she was conscious of the clip clop noise her soles made on what appeared to be a highly polished surface, one she was utterly convinced could easily have served as a mirror. Of course her escort did proffer his arm at this stage but Rachel quite blatantly ignored his offers of help determined that if she was forced to enter this building then she would do so under her own steam.

Once inside and through those revolving doors she was confronted with a lift which appeared to be the only feasible way that one could possibly access the inner chambers of the place, and she began to wonder what she had let herself in for. What exactly was this place anyway and who were these people whom Brett had stipulated wanted to meet her? Turning her head she noticed that Brett had now attached a badge to the lapel of his suit jacket, and after briefly stopping at the janitor's station he had apparently acquired another for herself, this one bearing the grand title of 'visitor' This of course contrasted with Brett's own badge which bore his name and somewhat wickedly she wondered if all these people needed a name badge simply remind themselves just who they were!

"Well put in on!" He motioned to the object almost impatiently and then made sure she obliged by motioning that if she did not oblige he would do the task for her. "Now we have to catch the lift!" By this time he had broken the frivolities of her thought pattern and yet again her attention became focussed upon the conveyance he indicated and even as Brett made to call upon its services she regretted his action for this would mean she would have to stand closer to him whilst conveyed to the appropriate floor and by this time she had taken objection to being here at all.

Leaving the lift yet another corridor faced them until finally her escort called a halt outside of one of the chambers before ushering her inside. Now she was given to wonder if all such meetings were held in the style of some government enquiry back at home with its semi-circle of chairs and a space for her to sit facing a sea of faces that now examined her appearance somewhat critically, almost indeed as if she was some sort of alien being. She remembered seeing such enquiries on the television back at home when the person called before the enquiry had been made to squirm. She realised Brett was sat alongside of her when he passed her a pair of earphones and motioned to her to put them on. Her initial reaction as to why she should want to wear these dratted objects was soon replaced by the feeling that if these people desired to question her then why could such politicians not speak in the Queen's English instead of babbling away in their own native tongues. At least when she had attended such a set up before with Callum the enquiry had possessed the manners to speak in the language that they were all familiar with. The trouble was that she wanted to get out of this place and the sooner the better and therefore she felt that perhaps in her own interest she had better pander to the status quo and accept the translation.

"We would first of all like to express our thanks to you for coming here!" After clearing his throat it seemed that it was time for one of these faceless ones to extend a greeting in her direction at which point Rachel could have laughed out loud for under the circumstances she had been given very little choice in the matter and therefore the decision to come here had not been something that she had been allowed to toy with! Still the person who had greeted her continued in a rather monotone voice "We believe Miss Burton that you have recently been in contact with your brother!"

For a moment she did wonder whether this was a case of playing happy families but then quickly changed her mind for after all Brett had previously warned her of this pending question although why he had to bring her to this place only to subject her to a question about her brother was a different matter.

"Briefly I suppose the answer to that is yes although at the moment I do not relish speaking of the circumstances that led to such a meeting!"

"We are already aware of the circumstances Miss Burton!" So Brett had done his homework well by acquainting them with the facts surrounding that meeting had he? "The matter that appears to us to be of greater concern is exactly what you were to learn from this encounter?"

"Perhaps the most important thing I learnt was the fact that my brother was still in the land of the living not having seen him for some considerable time!"

Her answer was obviously not well appreciated for her questioner gave her a look of exasperation whilst Brett amplified matters by kicking her across the shins under the table an action that succeeded in goading her into continuing. "Perhaps I should explain that my brother, after gaining a place at Oxford decided to change his status to a University in France and it was whilst he was there that he could often be found in the company of shall we say some deviates from the norm and consequently he was able to amass certain information that some may regard as nonsense!" She noticed one of the listeners shift suddenly and wondered whether this was the Frenchman who believed she was now decrying his beloved country and this thought quite frankly amused her.

"Please carry on!" The chairperson at least now appeared to show more sympathy towards her story and she wondered what nationality he was. Still there appeared to be nothing for it but to spell out the rest of the story.

"From what I was able to discern the group my brother presently associates with appear to have some far-fetched notions that there is a quantity of gold treasure still hidden somewhere in the region of the Cape Verde Islands. The story goes that some of the privateers in the days of good Queen Bess decided to off load a quantity of the spoils that they had gained through the wars with the Spaniards at that time somewhere on one of those Islands and consequently they did not return all their spoils of war to their Queen. One of those mentioned who apparently had quite a large part to play in this operation was Sir Francis Drake and for good measure the man is still regarded as being something of a pirate by the Islanders even in this century. Still even though the position of such buried treasure has not yet been established, the knowledge of this possibility has been enough to persuade several of our present day financiers to seek to invest their funds in its discovery. Thus finances that should have been supporting the Eurozone crisis have recently been withdrawn from the market. A matter I think you will concur which is enough to stir more than a little dissatisfaction amongst their colleagues. That I am afraid is all that I can tell you about the matter, apart from the fact that my own brother appears to be involved!"

"Thank you Miss Burton!" The chairman nodded his thanks before turning to his colleagues in an effort to enquire whether they had any more questions for the girl. Brett however seemed to seize the opportunity to step into the breach.

"I can verify Miss Burton's story for the meeting with her brother came as quite a surprise to her and she had little time to question the man further!"

"Of course but there again you do realise I hope that the I.M.F are currently finding themselves in the position of having to ask the Eurozone nations to support our fund to a greater degree. If indeed the girl is right and certain financiers have already removed their capital from out of the monetary measures of the countries involved then we will be heading for some difficulty in attempting to raise such funds as we require in order that we might assist our failing nations within the union!"

"I think that all countries will have difficulty in having to find the extra amounts you now want to perceive being placed at your disposal. I can hardly see my own government wishing to partake in this old boys club especially when one considers their own present economic needs!" It seemed apparent that Brett now found that he was rather uncomfortable with this argument.

"But there again your country has not yet lost its triple A star rating and is thus considered to be one of the more wealthier countries in the Eurozone. In addition to which I believe that some arrangement was previously made for your country to assist the I.M.F. should the need arise!"

"But not to the amount quoted in recent communications. My government most certainly could not pass that amount of money to this illustrious body without the permission of Parliament. And that I suggest would be quite difficult especially at a time when most of the population are feeling rather aggrieved with Europe and if a Referendum was called tomorrow the general populace would probably vote to opt out of the union altogether!"

His words had obviously given the committee some food for thought and glancing at his now reddened cheeks Rachel was of the impression that his verbatim had not dome much for Brett either. Her thoughts on the matter were to be verified when Brett moved as if he intended to leave the meeting.

"If you have finished with Miss Burton I suggest that I escort her back to her apartment before we proceed further on the matter!"

In truth the assembly did not appear to be in any hurry to let him go however. "Perhaps you had better reconsider Mr Chaplain for I believe that we have still much more to discuss!"

"But not I suggest in front of the lady for that in itself would be against the rules for she is not after all an elected member of this chamber!"

"Then can we presume that you will return after escorting Miss Burton back to her domain? We require your word on that of course Chaplain!"

"I believe that I have always previously abided by my word!" Now on his feet Brett was motioning her to stand, a motion which Rachel was only too keen to oblige apart from the fact that she had forgotten to remove her headphones destined for translation from around her ears, an act that at least served to break some of the tension that was currently present in that room. Still she sensed his relief once they finally managed to escape from the forum.

"Now you wouldn't be using me as a means to escape would you?" At least there was some degree of merriment in her eyes at the thought of those strangers' faces when she had become entangled with the blasted electronic cables.

"Why would you ever suggest anything like that? You forget those are my colleagues the people I am elected to work with!"

"In that case I feel rather sorry for you!"

"Why?"

"Because in my entire career dealing with economics I do not think I have ever met so many folk with such blinkered vision!"

"You are probably right in that assumption but there again it is the cross that I must bear!"

They had left the building by this time but Brett was obviously in no hurry to escort her back to her apartment. "If they want to wait for me then they are at liberty to do so. Although knowing that bunch they will have already deviated by this time. As far as you are concerned you have acquainted them with what you know and now I believe it is my duty to show you some of the sights of Brussels!"

"You mean that you will take me to where Callum now is?"

"Sorry Rachel but that is not my brief. On the other hand I feel sure that Callum already knows that you are present in the city and therefore if he wishes to get in touch with you then it is his prerogative to make the first move!"

"But that is not fair!"

"There is nothing that is fair in politics Rachel merely things that are expedient. Maybe that is a difficult thing for you to understand but nevertheless it is the truth!"

Rachel lapsed into silence. It was apparently true that Brett had no immediate intention of going back to attend that forum and instead had every intention of showing her something of the city. But to Rachel's mind this was not enough for she had come here to help him out in the expectation that this at least would lead to a reunion with Callum but now it appeared that she was being denied this opportunity!

The meeting when the occasion did finally arrive was almost accidental. After leaving the building with its glossy marble frontage and commencing upon a sightseeing tour of the city Rachel became more and more conscious of those blasted sandals rubbing against her feet. So much so that by the time the hour approached for her to return to her apartment she was in the throes of pathetically limping, whilst at the same time firmly believing that she must have parted with much of the skin from off her toes. Even so at the same time she fully believed that now she had stated her party piece to those men all dressed in the appropriate charcoal suits, the time was now rapidly approaching when she would be allowed to return to England and to these ends she was desperately seeking the comfort of those flats that had cosseted her feet when she had travelled here..

"If your feet are really troubling you that much then you will have to go out and find something different to wear!" Her escort however did not appear to be blessed with clemency over the matter. "And whilst you are about it you might as well get other articles that you will need during your stay!"

"But surely there is now no reason for me to stay here. After all I have told your friends all that I knew in answer to their questions therefore I cannot see any point in me staying here any longer, especially when I consider that I am neglecting my own work back at home!"

"I will say one thing and that is your memory appears to be remarkably short. You were brought here in the first place for your own safety and so far I have heard nothing that persuades me that it is safe for you to return home at the moment. Don't worry as soon as I am convinced that the danger to you no longer lurks behind closed doors I will see to it that you return back to that dreary little office where you appear to find comfort! In the meantime you might just as well make the most out of the situation and try to assimilate a little more knowledge about the city!" So saying this he then handed her a charge card. "Whatever you need to get then you charge it up to my account for there is no earthly reason why you should feel uncomfortable whilst you are here. Unfortunately as my own work depends a great deal on this place I won't be able to be with you every moment of the day and therefore having given you some idea of where various places are in the city I will have to trust you in my absence not to resort in trying anything that could be regarded as being foolish!"

He had left her at the apartment and Rachel did wonder whether he was about to return to that museum of technocrats although at the time her main priority had been to rid herself of those sandals and soak her feet into something that would soothe the damage she had accrued through walking in them.

It was indeed the next morning before she felt that her feet were capable of bearing her weight and knowing Brett was fully occupied with what people in his position were to paid to do she set out on a shopping spree, deciding that if she was to be kept here then she was going to use his card to its full advantage.

Thus finally laden with parcels and in the act of returning back to the apartment perhaps the last person she expected to spot was the figure of one Portuguese man, hardly in her terms fit to be called a gentleman. At first she believed that he had spotted her and immediately her heart sank for this was really something she could well do without but after spending a moment reflecting on the situation whilst at the same time doing her best to hide herself behind the wealth of things she had recently purchased, she soon became aware that the man was ignorant of her own presence for at that time Pablo Capello who appeared to be accompanied by yet another figure seemed to be currently in the process of following someone else.

It could be said that Rachel was nothing if not a little curious about this situation and moreover being Rachel, whether she was struggling with parcels or otherwise, she decided to follow at a discreet distance in the hope that if the man turned round he would not spot her especially if she employed the parcels to obscure her features.

Yet there was something strangely familiar about the other person's features who was currently with Capello, and as light dawned on her as to whom this person was Rachel took an involuntary step backwards before willing herself to step forward once again. For the person who now accompanied Capello so happened to be her own brother and if she was not very much mistaken the pair was in the act of now attempting to follow Callum himself. Indeed it now appeared to her that the pair had been waiting for the man to appear from out of one of those gaunt buildings that housed the European diplomats.

There could be little doubt that Rachel was in a state of shock at spotting her brother and his reasons for being there. But then she supposed that he had been at Greta's apartment on the fated evening and Greta of course was well acquainted with Pablo Capello. But why on earth the pair appeared to be now in the process of trying to trail Callum was a different matter and something that she could not answer. Neither come to that could she come to terms with why Brett had befriended her in that manner if his former colleagues were in town, although in all fairness there was nothing to support the fact that Greta was here and Pablo could have been present on Eurozone matters. That of course still did not explain to her why her brother was now here and why the two of them appeared intent upon following Callum. It was a thought that brought to mind that she herself was also in search of Callum and which possibly obscured the reality of the two other individuals currently situated between her and the man whom she sought.

Perhaps Rachel had long prided herself on her inventiveness but before she could think of a possible deviation, her opportunity arose through natural circumstances. It came in the form of a series of police whistles over a traffic incident but it was something that acted in drawing the two men's attention away from their quarry: That was when Rachel seized the opportunity to mingle with the crowds and pass them by. Upon reaching Callum's side she was breathless and had only enough strength to blurt out the words. "You are being followed!" before she almost collapsed upon him through lack of air.

If Callum had not expected to see her he at least acted quickly upon her words by pushing her through the doors of one of the popular Belgian cafes and then after grabbing her parcels from out of her hand he motioned her to a table that was situated towards the rear of the place and where they could not be seen from the street.

"When you've caught up your breath perhaps you will be good enough to explain to me what the hell you are doing here and then perhaps tell me what it is that you are talking about!" The tone of his voice appeared to be quite blunt and certainly nothing like the voice of the Callum she remembered.

"The reason why I happen to be here, apart that is from trying to find you, can wait. But after spotting you in the street I considered it right to seize the opportunity to warn you that you were being followed by Pablo Capello!"

"You say followed but then the man has a perfect right to be here in Brussels at this time and therefore I consider it to be a misapprehension on your part!"

"Not so if his actions were anything to go by. He also had a male companion with him!" She bit her lip for she had not wanted to speak about her brother.

"By that I presume you mean your brother?" The waitress had come over to the table and Callum ordered the coffee without looking at her to see the reaction on her face.

"Yes!" Her voice sounded warped and twisted as she admitted the truth. But then her brother, whatever else he was, happened to be her own kith and kin. "I have certainly not seen my brother for ages until a few nights ago when I had reason to discover that he was involved in some way with fanciful notions about the Eurocrats seeking to invest their capital in Drake's gold!" Perhaps she expected to see him surprised with her words but if he was then Callum certainly did not show it.

"I have no doubt that he will have found the perfect foil in Capello for such activities especially if there is no one present to keep an eye on him. But you have not yet explained why you are here in Belgium. I had presumed that by this time you would have been flaunting your recently acquired articles?"

"I probably failed my board because I was more intent on finding out what had happened to you. Perhaps a phone call to assure me that you were all right would have helped for as it was nobody would tell me anything about the accident nor where you were or what you were doing until I heard by chance that you had been sent to this place!"

"There was nothing to tell and anyway my work here is strictly confidential and one that requires me to go solo. So although I am grateful for your concern you were really worrying unduly!" He paused as the coffee arrived on the table. "So tell me what inspired you to finally come to Belgium?" He glanced at the parcels she had been carrying. "Surely you are not on a shopping trip?"

"No I left England under some duress and consequently I needed some clothes to change into!"

"I take it then that the purchase of such articles was necessary in order to relieve this duress you speak about? Yet you are still wearing a suit upon which I commend your choice?"

"One that Brett provided me with so that I could attend the meeting he had arranged. But as he brought me here for my own security or so I was told, and I have been informed that I will be staying for some time, something that I cannot argue about as the man still has my passport, he decided that I could probably do with additions!"

"You say that Brett Chaplain was responsible for bringing you here?" Once again the tone of his voice had changed and Rachel could now sense a tenet of disapproval ringing within it.

"Yes, he brought me here for my own safety after I had an entanglement with Greta Silvio!"

"And you did not think it strange that this man should act as your rescuer considering the friendship which the two of them had at one time apparently shared?"

"Maybe it does sound a little unusual but at least I believe that Brett saved my life by getting me away from that woman and her henchmen!"

"And what else did he require of you for this favour. What was his other reason?"

"I attended a meeting with the I.M.F. with him if that is what you mean!"

"And for what reason did you do that?" His face still remain stern as if he was resenting all she had to tell him and Rachel swallowed hard for it was not easy for her even at this stage to implicate her brother!

"I informed them of what I had recently discovered about my brother's activities!" She sighed, for much as she hated the thought of implicating her brother she wanted no falsehoods to lie between herself and Callum. The man now appeared an enigma but doubtless he had his reasons and what was more Rachel remembered the feelings that they had once shared, and this was a feeling that she still felt deeply about.

"Let me get this right, you attended a meeting of the I.M.F merely to inform them of this matter. Did it never occur to you that such an august body would have probably known about the matter even before you attended their little gathering? I am afraid Rachel that it appears that you are meddling in things that do not really concern you and therefore the only advice I can now offer you is to get your passport back and return to England as soon as it is possible!"

"But what of yourself Callum? After all my main motivation for coming here was to try and establish some form of contact with you?"

"I am afraid that I have now got my own agenda to follow. Look Rachel we did well together when you acted as my stenographer and girl Friday at those previous meetings. But the cruise and all it entailed is over with now therefore meddling in matters that do not concern you is hardly going to help the on-going situation in this place. Therefore I consider that the best thing you can do is to return back to England and try your best to persuade your Board to give you a second chance!"

He suddenly stood and Rachel quickly became aware that his intentions were now to leave the café whilst refusing to answer any more questions. Half of her wanted to call him back to tell him that she had no intention to interfere with his work and to beg him to tell her what had happened after he had been injured and that the last thing she wanted was to go back to England and meet her Board again. But then Rachel was not without pride and therefore whilst his words had stung her like some unsuspected nettle hidden in a field of green pasture she did not speak out but merely watched as he left the café without even giving a backward look in her direction.

After that there seemed to be little else she could do but return back to the apartment with her parcels. Baggage that was still left unopened upon Brett's return as she sat trying to come to terms with what had happened in her own mind.

"Well that's nice I must say. I give you my card to go out and get yourself some new clothes to wear and you haven't even opened the parcels?" Perhaps the man was a little incredulous as he noted her bearing when he returned.

"I thank you for the use of your card but the shopping trip was not after all without incident!"

Brett regarded her in serious mode as he waited for her to continue and perhaps much against the grain she knew that she must.

"I actually spotted two people I would rather not have seen in the shopping mall after I had made my purchases!"

"And they were?" He found it necessary to prompt her before she would continue.

"Pablo Capello, together with my brother Steven: At the time they were following another person. I was fortunate in the sense that a traffic incident diverted their attention and I was able to get past them and warn the person that they were following!" She had still not mentioned Callum by name. "You needn't worry for I am sure that they didn't see my action!"

"So who was the person you felt duty bound to warn?"

"It was Callum!" Now there was no longer any escape from telling the truth.

"And? You saw Callum; you went to warn him that he was being followed, what happened then?"

"Not a great deal. I was advised to return to England. His work here obviously doesn't involve me!" Perhaps a tinge of bitterness had crept into her voice for Brett eyed her sternly.

"And what exactly did you expect? After all this is a far different world to life on a cruise liner Rachel.

"Perhaps I thought that I at least deserved some explanation as to why he had never contacted me. Maybe under the circumstances he was right. Perhaps I should return to England for after all if Capello and Steven are here in Brussels then they will hardly pose any threat back home!"

"But Greta is not here so apparently she is still back in England. I thought that we had an understanding, I brought you here so that you would be safe from the woman's talons?" At any other time it might have sounded strange for Brett to describe the woman in this vein but then Rachel was not thinking of other times at that moment. "You also forget Rachel that I am holding onto your passport and therefore you will not return to that place until I decide that it is safe for you to do so. And now having purchased the clothes you require maybe you could undo those parcels and we can see what you got!" He indicated the still wrapped parcels lying untouched on the table. "Well come on girl, for the life of me I guess I will never understand the mind of woman!"

*   *   *   *

Chapter Nine

If Rachel thought for one moment that she had seen the back of Brett Chaplain after she had tried on those clothes and perambulating like some sort of manikin in front of him, albeit in a very disgruntled fashion, then she was to be mistaken. She had realised of course that he had been on his mobile whilst she had been in her bedroom in the act of changing but after reluctantly admiring her choice of garments to wear during her enforced stay he announced that another matter had suddenly come up behaving as if some other business had now commanded his attention.

"I don't suppose you will remember Senor Gonzalaz from the meeting we attended yesterday?"

"Why, should I?" She was still in a disgruntled manner when she answered him, upset about Callum's attitude towards her earlier on that day and feeling bloody minded that after carrying out his bidding, her present escort refused to let her return to England. "You confront me with a sea of faces and whilst you might be familiar with them and are able to recite their names by rote they mean little to me!"

"As a matter of fact I have just been speaking to him on the phone and he wishes to meet up with you again!" Brett deliberately ignored her comments intent as he was at getting his own message across.

"I know that you have been on the telephone but as to who rang who in the first place I do not know. Anyway why does this man want to see me, haven't I already told them all that I know about my brother's activities?"

"But that was before you spotted him with Pablo Capello today here in Brussels!"

"Then perhaps you should be the one to go and meet this person. After all you appeared to know a great deal about Capello's movements at one time, that is of course, along with your friend from that period, I am speaking now of Greta Silvio!" She was determined not to lend him any assistance in this matter for in truth she was beginning to feel sick of the whole situation that kept reverberating back and left her with little peace of mind. Maybe this feeling however had again been inspired by Callum's attitude towards her earlier on that day for his mood had certainly been subjected to something that she could not easily reconcile to herself.

"And that is what you think? You really believe that I was attached to Greta and not merely using such an opportunity in an attempt to learn more about their little game?"

"If you weren't attached to the woman then you could have fooled me for you acted that way even when she stood you up for her Portuguese boyfriend!"

"A convenient ploy, and a move moreover you helped to provide me with the opportunity to carry out. After all there was only one girl that I would have preferred to have become attached to on that boat but she appeared to have her eyes firmly fixed elsewhere. Therefore I utilised the opportunity, which conveniently presented itself, to glean more about a certain movement!"

"And that, I suppose, you would have me believe? Really Brett, please credit me with a little more intelligence than that!"

"Then ask yourself why I saw fit to rescue you from the clutches of one rather evil woman if I had been in league with her all the time?" At least he had managed to pose a question that had flummoxed her and after a moments silence she then attempted to change the subject.

"So what does your little man want to see me about?"

"He takes the matter of your brother now being in the company of Pablo Capello rather seriously and therefore the Senor would like to learn a little more from your own lips as to what exactly happened this afternoon. Therefore I took the liberty of saying that we would meet with him in the morning. Don't worry, this is but one man not the entire delegation that you will have to face up to and I have also arranged for you to meet him in a neutral place!"

“And I suppose that I don’t have any say in the matter?”

“Not really for you see you happen to be involved in all of this right up to your pretty little neck!”

“I am not my brother’s keeper if that is what you are inferring! In fact I know very little about his associates since he decided to opt out of his studies at Oxford!” She squared her shoulders almost defiantly at her companion. Not that Brett appeared to have noticed this action for he seemed to be far more intent on the mission in hand.

“I said that we would see him around eleven o’clock therefore as you now appear to be in something of a mood I will pick you up about ten thirty”. And then as she shrugged in a rather non-committal way. “Look I am sorry if you got little change out of Callum when you met him, but the two of us work for entirely different departments over here and sometimes our departments do not agree on matters even when we are trying in our own way to promote the same ideals!”

“The way I feel at the moment is quite frankly I don’t give a damn even if you are avowed enemies! But one thing I am sure about is that it was your so-called friends that dealt that blow to Callum on the quayside in Lisbon!” It was intended to be her final rejoinder before he left but in truth she was still feeling quite bewildered at what had transpired that day with Callum showing her a cold shoulder and now Brett trying to claim that his association with Greta had been fortuitous and had been brought about by her own dismissal of him. To her mind this sort of explanation seemed to be a little too far-fetched to bear any resemblance to the truth and the truth was something that she was now determined to find out!

Even so her words resulted in Brett pausing in the doorway before he left. "Whatever you think, and whilst I admit the man is something of a scoundrel, it was not Capello who landed Callum that blow in Portugal!"

"You seem to be pretty certain of your facts!" Rachel remembered that this was not the first time she had heard that claim. "Then if it wasn't Pablo after I had left them arguing on the quayside who was it then?"

"Sorry but there are more things that meet the eye Rachel and maybe Callum is the one who can answer your question more succinctly. But whatever else he happens to be, please remember that Pablo still happens to be a diplomat and I doubt very much that he would resort to taking such action against another Euro state member!"

"Yet your diplomatic friend was still responsible for the death of that girl Martha on the boat. The one that Adri was apportioned the blame for!"

"Again you have no reason to suppose that. After all Cqpello was not on the boat at the time it happened!"

"So it appears one is led to believe! Then perhaps you can explain how your friend managed to get those scratch marks down his face especially after the autopsy revealed that the girl had struggled with her attacker and more to the point flakes of skin were found under her nails!"

"There is one thing about you Rachel and that is you never cease to exercise your vivid imagination. But that is enough I will see you in the morning!"

"Before you leave then tell me why am I left with the impression that you and Callum do not see eye to eye on most matters? After all, your attitude towards each other on the boat could hardly be determined as being friendly?" Perhaps it was a shot in the dark but Rachel was soon aware that her words had certainly found their target.

"Perhaps you should consider that there was one certain girl involved at the time!" His reply was terse and the impression that his words gave immediately informed her that this was one matter that Brett was not prepared to talk about.

Thus Brett took his leave without further explanation and Rachel was left to suffer a sleepless night as her mind toyed over and over again with the events of the day in an ill-fated attempt to provide some logical conclusion. Thus when the morning came and the sound of the alarm clock informed her that it was time to arise it was therefore a rather weary Rachel who fumbled her way into the bathroom to make some attempt to repair the ravages of her face.

The man she was to meet that morning, she had to admit, appeared on first impression to be both kind and courteous and certainly not of the mind to subject her any third degree like she had half expected and. Rachel wondered why she did not remember him from the delegation she had attended, but then guessed that at the time facing her had been a sea of faces that had all appeared to be determined to catch her out. Now however Senor Gonzalez was able to put a different complexion on matters.

"Of course we have met before my dear! I am meaning before yesterday!" This remark came as a follow up to the introductions once they had taken place. "At that time you were acting as aide to Senor Rothwell whilst you were on Gran Canaria. I was invited to attend because that place so happens to be my home and consequently I am a native of the Canaries. I remember that Pablo Capello was present and also that he persisted in making something of a nuisance of himself and now I believe from what you told us that he is not only here in Brussels, which one supposes that as a diplomat he has a right to be, but that he is also accompanied by your brother who also appears to have some rather outlandish theories but ones nevertheless we feel sure that Capello might be tempted to use in order to promote his own ends!"

"I told you yesterday everything that I knew about my brother's ideology concerning Drake's gold. I cannot tell you where he managed to glean such ideas from except that he was in Paris for some time after switching his studies from Oxford for reasons of his own!"

"Ah the ides of youth! But then we have heard rumours of such ideas being percolated through some of the learning establishments of that city. Yet there is a difference between young men playing games of make-belief between themselves and others taking the matter seriously enough to attempt to involve financiers' money in their quest, merely because they have been led to believe that investing their finances in the Euro is a rather risky matter in the present financial climate. Moreover the fact that one of these young would be entrepreneurs has been spotted in the company of Pablo Capello has now also placed a rather serious complexion on the matter, for our man from Portugal is not into playing games especially without ensuring some sort of recompense for himself!"

"When I spotted them they appeared to be following Callum Rothwell and at the time I would say that they wished to be unobserved!"

"A factor that makes the matter all the more interesting: Tell me though Miss Burton, are you in contact with your brother?"

"I am most definitely not!" Rachel's vehement response caused the Spaniards eyebrows to be raised but then the man was not a diplomat for nothing.

"In that case I take it that you would have no objection to us taking matters into our own hands?"

"I have no objections!" Rachel shivered as she thought back to her meeting with Steven at Greta's apartment. "There is also one other factor to be taken into consideration. I have good reason to believe that my brother has also an association with Greta Silvio who in turn also appears to be on amicable terms with Capello!"

"Ah yes I believe I remember the woman. She acted as stenographer for Capello at the conference we attended in Las Palmas. One could hardly forget the woman with those ridiculously painted finger nails!" Rachel preened herself upon his words for at least it appeared that she had not been on her own in recognising those talons.

"The same!" She felt Brett stiffen besides her but now she couldn't care a jot what she said about the woman. After all she was the one who had attempted to keep Rachel incarcerated in that place and that factor alone was probably the least relevant in the case against her.

"I think that you can rest assured that we will deal with the matter Miss Burton for undermining the attempts of the Eurozone to relieve us from this economic crisis is the last thing that we need at the present time. I would like to take this opportunity to thank you for your help in this matter!" The man had all the charm of a Spaniard as he took her hand to deftly place his lips upon it, much to Brett's annoyance. In fact for once Rachel almost appreciated the funny side of this scenario. But after the his salute the Spaniard took his leave beaming a smile of reassurance in her direction and Rachel could not bear to see Brett's face at this stage in case she burst out laughing.

But what was she doing? Rachel suddenly chided herself for she was in no laughing mood. Laughter was hardly likely to provide the answers she was still seeking, perhaps of Brett's own role but most definitely answers about Callum and what he was now purporting to be doing!

"You seem to have made a conquest. I suppose that was only to be expected from one of minx like qualities!"

This time she did look in his direction with anger flaring in her eyes. "Then if you consider that I have minx like qualities Brett Chaplain, what exactly does that make you?"

"Perhaps you could consider that it makes me someone who is about to take you out to lunch as I now find myself at a loose end!" She was now conscious that Brett refused to take her question seriously and for once Rachel swallowed her pride after promising herself that the time of reckoning with this man had still to come but at the moment it unfortunately needed to be left in abeyance.

Nor could she find fault with his impeccable behaviour over the meal, all of which served to irritate her further, for Rachel now wanted to speak about Callum and his protracted sense of behaviour towards her. In short the girl wanted to know why he was acting in this way. But of course Brett was not impervious to his escort's mood and it was over coffee that he finally moved to goad the truth out of her.

"I guess then by your demeanour that the man is still on your mind?"

"Of course for one thing I cannot understand his change of attitude upon seeing me!"

"Then what exactly did he say?"

"He went to great lengths to tell me that the cruise was over with now and a past entity!"

"And of course he was right. If it will help you at all I have heard that Callum is shortly to depart for Strasburg. Apparently there is a difference of opinion between his master and the court of human rights that appear to be over-ruling our own country's judiciary rather too frequently of late. And of course when his master whistles for his presence on affairs of state then Callum has little alternative other than to obey his commander!"

"What exactly did you mean back there when you stated that it wasn't Pablo who hit Callum on the head that day?"

"You require to know a great deal Rachel therefore please do not jump to the wrong conclusions when I tell you that in his line of work Callum associates with many people sometimes of both sexes. I am led to believe that it just happened to be the boyfriend of one of these female contacts who did not approve of such a relationship. In a nutshell the man presumed rightly or wrongly that something had been going on between his intended and the English agent and consequently he blew a short fuse. In all probability after that Callum received a stern warning over his activities when he returned to the U.K which possibly resulted in the reception you received from him.. But tell me something, why should I worry about that man, especially as we have never seen eye to eye about anything so far?"

"I'm sorry but I find your explanation a little difficult to believe. Also if the pair of you are supposed to work for the same government then why is there this apparent animosity between the two of you?"

"Maybe you ought to ask Greta about that. As a matter of fact she has just come into the café!" Upon mention of the woman's name Rachel stiffened for now she really did not know what was supposed to be going on!"

"Don't worry for you are perfectly safe here with me. Remember I have still to explain why I resorted to brandishing a Taser in her place!"

Perhaps it was fortunate that Rachel did not have time to worry or even ponder about the woman's presence here for Greta was in the process of advancing towards their table and the advent of that person in any place was enough to stifle the atmosphere.

"Ah Gregg darling I was wondering where you had got to!" If Rachel had been worried about her presence the woman in return appeared determined to completely ignore her at least for the moment. Indeed the only thing Rachel was aware of were those talons that even now were sneaking their way around Brett's neck as she planted a perfunctory kiss upon his face. "You were rather naughty however when you took your leave of me in England threatening me with that weapon but of course I will forgive you, after of course some slight consideration!"

"I suppose you are aware that Pablo is present here in Brussels at the moment?" Brett obviously sought to ignore her phraseology maybe he felt a little embarrassed at Rachel's presence with Greta flaunting her arms around his neck.

"But of course I am aware that he is here. After all that is the reason why I am here myself! Naturally Pablo has every right to be in this city and that is why I sent your brother out to meet him!" With her final words

Greta turned her attention onto Rachel for perhaps the first time. "Indeed it would appear that Brett provided a service in bringing you here my dear for it is dreadfully difficult for one to attempt to conduct dealings in two countries at the same time, but now it appears that we are all in the same city together. No doubt you will have also seen that Callum is here as well?"

Rachel remained silent for there was literally no way that she would admit to having seen the man to this person and Greta laughed almost sardonically in her direction.

"Your silence informs me that you have seen him my dear; so tell me how was he after his ordeal?"

"I only met him briefly really in a manner of passing and therefore I was unable to ask him anything appertaining to his health. Indeed I have reason to believe that he has now left for Strasbourg!"

"But of course for the boy takes his work very seriously. On the other hand perhaps his absence could prove to be a bonus for I do not consider the man will do us any harm whilst he is in that place admiring the ones who wear wigs! The immediate matter however is for me to now contact Pablo. I guess it is imperative that we now find a use for that boy with his outlandish ideas and I have no doubt that Pablo will already have had thoughts on this matter. Oh but I am so sorry my dear I guess I forgot for a moment that the boy was your brother!" She turned towards Rachel with what appeared to be a sickening smile and the latter had few doubts that such a sentence had been passed for her benefit. Yet Rachel was certainly not for admitting that she had also seen her brother together with Pablo and the only thought in her head at the time had been one borne more from disgust than anything else.

"Until recent days I have had very little contact with my brother as you must be well aware!" Rachel had the satisfaction of seeing the woman draw her talons in almost indeed as if she was ready to pounce. But this, she obviously felt was not the time to pursue matters that had happened in the past and therefore Rachel witnessed the forced smile that gelled her lips before she responded.

"But of course, I am afraid that I had forgotten!"

Perhaps it was then when Brett decided to intervene. "Rachel has in fact been of great assistance to my colleagues in recent days!"

"I admit that I am glad that she has proved to be of some service to you. And there was I believing that her prime motivation in coming to Brussels was to seek out Callum. After all she was distraught upon the man's disappearance and demanded to know some answers!" Again Greta was attempting to prove provocative.

"You said that you had come here in order to meet Pablo. Was there a special reason then for this visit for I am quite sure you did not come all this way on account of one boy?" At last Brett had appeared to come to her rescue by attempting to change the subject and Rachel now cast a glance of thanks in his direction.

"But of course there is a special reason for my presence here. Surely you do not envisage that I left England on the whims of one eccentric child do you?"

Brett glanced at her in speculation and Greta, not being one that refused an opportunity to flaunt herself gave him a half smile in return. "I believe that there is another summit on the agenda and although it will be for his chief minister to attend in person I have no doubt that the man will welcome the input we can offer to him. Plus in addition I believe that Pablo relies a great deal on my judgement in such matters!" Greta examined her nails again and Rachel wondered whether the woman, now bored with the conversation, was ready to reach for her nail file.

"Then no doubt you will be anxious to find him?" Brett surprised her with his handling of the situation but then the man seemed to be almost as eager to part with the woman's presence as what Rachel did herself.

"But of course and for that reason I must beg you to excuse me although no doubt we will have the opportunity of continuing this interesting discourse at some future date!"

Rachel breathed a sigh of relief as she realised the woman was about to take her leave although in truth she considered that Brett watched Greta's departure with mixed feelings. Indeed his face held something of a pensive look when she disappeared from their midst.

"So what is the matter, don't tell me that you are sorry that Greta had to make a hasty departure?"

"I hadn't realised that another summit had been planned so soon!" The man still looked as if this was a factor he should have known about and not had to wait for the likes of someone like Greta telling him but

Rachel's thoughts were already racing on ahead so much so that she ignored the other's hesitance.

"Then if there is to be a summit meeting will that mean that Callum will be there?" Her one thought now was to see the man and try to sort out whatever difference had occurred between them.

"In all probability, that is if he has finished the task he was sent to complete in Strasbourg, for I expect the P.M. will want to see him before any such meeting takes place. But if you have any thoughts of attempting to interrupt him on this quest then I should forget it Rachel!" Once again Brett's expression had turned stern.

"Why, when I believe I have a right to know the truth from him?" Now the girl appeared adamant.

"Then you do not believe anything that you have heard today!"

"I'm afraid that I would like the matter clarified!" She remembered how much the man had meant to her and how she had believed that her feelings had been reciprocated. Now she needed to know the truth and there was only one person who could provide her with the answers to this.

"Rachel I don't want to see you get hurt. Remember your brother and the role he is playing in all of this. What do you think Callum would have to say about that?"

"I have already said that I am not my brother's keeper and as such I cannot let him interfere with my life!" The girl was adamant in her intentions and Brett realised that he would now have to change his tack

"Rachel sometimes I despair of you. Perhaps if I did not care so much about you it would make life a little easier. Still considering that another summit now appears to be in the offing I now find that there are matters that I must attend to. Therefore if you don't mind I will return you to the comparative safety of your apartment whilst I attend to such matters and we will resume this conversation at a later stage. In fact I will reserve a table for us at Toni's if you like!"

"Under the circumstances it might possibly prove to be more prudent if you returned my passport and then I can go back again home. After all the supposed risk that you believed that I was under now appears to have removed itself onto the continent!"

"And what if I said that I did not wish you to go. At least not until we have straightened out one or two matters between us?"

"As far as I can see there is nothing further for us to sort out. After all I have obliged you by meeting your colleagues. What else do you now want of me?"

"Perhaps we will discuss that matter later maybe after dinner, but you can be sure of one thing Rachel Burton and that is I happen to care about you a great deal!"

They lapsed into an uneasy silence on the way back to her apartment. The thought of Brett proving to be an additional complication in her life had not previously occurred to her, nor did she even want to even consider it. Therefore when he finally left her Rachel paced the apartment wondering on her role in handling this new situation for the last thing she felt she needed were additional complications at this stage.

Engrossed in her thoughts she did not at first hear the initial knock on her flat door not that was until the person who wanted to gain access decided to apply some force to the ringing of her doorbell. Dreading the thought that this could be Gregg who had returned earlier than expected she answered the call rather warily and then stopped short as her breath came in short gasps. For standing there was probably the last person she had expected to see and for his part Callum Rothwell pushed past her to gain admittance to the apartment almost as if he demanded the right to do so.

"I thought you had gone to Strasbourg!" This in all honesty was the only thing she could think of to say especially after the coolness he had shown towards her at their last encounter.

"I did go to Strasbourg that is correct but now I believe my presence is required back here. In point of fact I am due to meet with the P.M. prior to this new summit that has been called. My main reason for returning to this place and coming here to see you is to inform you that as your brother was considered to be something of a liability especially with this summit on the agenda I felt duty bound to take steps to have him removed and sent back to England with his passport then forfeited so that he will find it difficult to return back to the continent at the moment. I have come here merely to inform you of this fact for no one has any desire to see one misguided youth finding himself in even more trouble if he decides to intervene in the workings of the Eurozone!"

"Callum there is much for us to talk about. Things that I need to know----!"

"Then I must apologise for I am afraid that I have neither the time nor the inclination to oblige you. Besides you appear to have found some measure of consolation in Brett Chaplain and I am quite sure that he will find adequate words to explain the situation to you and thus satisfy your curiosity!"

"Callum what you are suggesting is simply not true for even if I feel that I do owe Gregg something for rescuing me back in England, it is you whom I want to talk to and nobody else!"

"Then I am sorry but at this moment I feel that I have neither the time nor the inclination to enter into your world of subterfuge. I came here merely to acquaint you with the facts appertaining to your brother and now that I have completed that task I will be on my way for my schedule happens to be pretty tight!"

He moved to the door leaving Rachel aghast to see him go. Surely this was not the same man that she had spent time with on that boat. The man whom she had fallen in love with? But Callum did not pause and when he left the room he had been in seemed to be suddenly void.

She was still pacing the place with her thoughts flying from one thing to another and a sickening feeling of rejection tightening the pit of her stomach when Brett returned.

"You haven't changed yet ready for dinner?" His eyes took in her dishevelled form in some disbelief. "I booked a table for us at Toni's remember?"

"Yes I -------!" She broke off for a moment as she remembered how she had decided to use this opportunity to try to persuade Brett to part with her passport. Strange how both siblings appeared to be having trouble with their passports at this time. "Callum called here to inform me that my brother has now been deported back to England and his passport forfeited!" The words issued forth almost in a rush but she supposed that she had to tell him and anyway the news seemed to simply flutter quite automatically from her lips.

"I thought I told you to forget all about that man. He is no good for you Rachel!"

"Please remember that he called on me and not the other way around. In addition he came simply to inform me about Steven!" She had no idea why it was that she still wanted to protect Callum and indeed what she was trying to protect him from.

"Possibly the departure of your brother is no bad thing under the circumstances although why Callum felt that he had the right to see to this without consultation is something else. So I presume you managed to discover why he hadn't contacted you before?"

Rachel shook her head, an action that appeared to spark some sign of relief on Brett's face. "No he stayed only for a couple of minutes for he claimed that he had already got a meeting therefore I didn't get the chance to ask him!" She crossed her fingers behind her back but there was literally no way that she was going to admit to Brett that Callum had appeared to be rather off-handish with her, nor that he had suggested that she had now turned her affections in Brett's direction. Yet again she was positive however that her words were received with some relief from Brett.

"Then I suggest you go and get yourself prettied up. Perhaps a night out will not do you any harm at all. In fact it might even make you feel more kindly towards me!"

She supposed that she had no alternative but to do what he had suggested and therefore out of fairness to the man who after all had done little to warrant her feelings of the blues, Rachel dressed carefully choosing a floor length cocktail dress that did much to enhance her figure and with her makeup carefully applied and her hair brushed back to rid it of its tell-tale knotted locks she reappeared looking well worth the time that had been spent in waiting for her.

Brett drew in his breath as she re-appeared before taking her arm. "Well worth the wait that is what I am thinking and tonight we will make a pact, I promise there will be no more talk about Callum and you can promise that you will forget all about your arguments over your passport. Have we got a deal then?"

Rachel nodded for it seemed to be the only way out. Besides she considered that Brett possibly deserved a little bit of attention, just so long as he got no ideas about anything else!

Even so the past sometimes has a peculiar way of being able to resurrect itself and usually at the most inappropriate moments. They were in fact in the midst of enjoying their meal at Toni's when the outside door opened to admit two more characters from off the street. One of these persons Rachel immediately recognised and she almost shouted out in surprise when the other person obviously recognised her too and came across to their table much she observed to Brett's annoyance.

"Adri, this is a pleasant surprise but I thought you would have left Brussels with your delegation long ago!"

"Not so Miss Rachel but there again perhaps I was waiting for my English friend to travel out to the continent once more!" Then seeing her expression the Croatian laughed. "No, our delegation that you assisted me in joining appeared to do well out here but then we learnt of the pending Eurozone summit and several of the members from the various states who are attending expressed a desire to meet with us, not at the summit meeting itself of course but privately whilst they were in the country. Therefore Dimitri and I were requested to stay behind after the delegation had returned to our mother country. I suspect that I was chosen because now I have a good command of the English and Dimitri was chosen so that he could keep an eye on me!" The Croatian laughed at his words and Rachel thought it refreshing to hear the young man making merry again after the trauma he had been put through. On the other hand if one regarded his expression at the time one could not have said that Brett shared her thoughts on this matter.

"I believe that we have you to thank for Adri being able to return to his own kin for which my country thanks you Miss!" Now it was Dimitri who solemnly shook her hand.

"But I really did little. Your friend was so upset about losing his Martha at the time ------!" It was Rachel who felt that she had to set the picture straight although whether she claimed she did little for Brett's benefit was a matter for conjecture for by this time her partner was shuffling his feet under the table rather impatiently.

"Ah yes, you speak of the poor girl whom Adri met on the boat!" Dimitri nodded as if he had already been informed of that relationship. "Adri was upset about the girl for a time yes, but then he has found someone in his own country, a girl I might say whom he had known for some time. So all is well that ends well, do you not think? But now Adri we must go for we are keeping these good people from enjoying their time together!"

For a moment Adri looked puzzled for he had not associated Rachel with this man before. This man was the one who had been fascinated with the one with those horrid finger nails, and the Croatian shivered as he thought of Greta. Then however he conceded that his friend was right and it was time for them to depart for Dimitri had concluded the business that they had with this place.

Perhaps Rachel had expected some sort of rejoinder after the two had left the place, a rejoinder that could have turned into a full blown argument if Brett Chaplain had not had other things on his mind at the time.

"Strange I thought the Croat said that he had stayed behind when the rest of the delegation left Brussels because he was the one with a good command of the English language. Listening to his friend however it would appear that he is also quite eloquent in speaking it. All of which serves to make one wonder!"

"As far as I can see there is only one thing to wonder about and that is why you always disliked the Croatian ever since we first met him!"

"I am inclined to reserve my judgement on that. The whole idea of tonight was to bring you out in order to attempt to break the sorry mood you appeared to be in just because you had seen Callum even if only fleetingly. It was certainly not to entertain foreigners who are not part of the Eurozone yet. Perhaps we need to change the subject. Perhaps indeed it is time for me to confess that one reason for me not giving you back your passport is because I simply want to keep you here. I did think when we were on the boat at the start of the voyage that we had something going between us. That of course was before that man Callum showed up. Perhaps after today you will concede how little he really felt about you, for if his feelings had been true then surely he would not have left you in such an abrupt manner!"

"He said that he had something urgent to see to!" She wondered whether she was now simply making excuses for Callum's attitude.

"In this city we have all got something to do Rachel. Contrary to popular belief the Eurocrats do not earn their money so easily, but that does not excuse one from being impolite to say the least. I have already told you to forget him Rachel and save having your heart broken. I have also told you about the other women he has wooed in the past. So why not turn to someone who really cares about you and who would like to play a larger role in your life?"

His hand had stretched across the table to encompass her own and Rachel forced a smile in his direction. Somehow it seemed to be a little unfair on the man when his intentions were obviously honourable to throw his goodwill back in his face. Yet she knew even then in her heart where her true love still lay even if that person had recently chosen to discard her!

⋆ ⋆ ⋆ ⋆

Chapter Ten

After spending until the early hours of the following morning with Rachel and finally believing that he was getting somewhere with the girl, the last thing Brett Chaplain desired as light began to invade the skies was to be woken up with a tirade of fierce knocking on his flat door and then after opening it, by this time partially convinced that there must be some major catastrophe and that the buildings had to be evacuated, to find the likes of Pablo Capello looking almost like the devil in a rage and demanding to be let in!

"All right what's the mad rush then?" Brett yawned as he ran his fingers through his still tousled hair.

"This summit meeting we have been called to attend!" The man in question pushed his way past Brett and into the flat showing no form of consideration.

"Well that has nothing to do with me for it's not my department that is involved. I wouldn't have thought that you would have been involved either for it seems to be only for heads of state and first ministers!"

"I know that. The truth of the matter is that my chief needs a stenographer and I have a good idea you are keeping one here at the moment!" Pablo looked past Brett possibly expecting to see Rachel making an ungainly appearance.

"If you are speaking of Rachel then rest assured she is not here, and as a point of interest we are not co-habiting. But I was under the impression that you already had someone who met the description of the person you seek in full, at least you went to great pains to give everyone the impression that was what Greta was, an accomplished stenographer?"

"The girl has refused to do it; that is she has refused to work for the boss. No doubt she is sitting on her high horse about something I have said or done, therefore I need to find an alternative body and mighty quick as well if I am to retain my own position!"

"And what makes you think that Rachel will co-operate? I seem to remember that she is hardly kindly disposed towards you!"

"Funnily enough I am under the impression that she will because I believe that you are going to be the one to persuade her, and please don't underestimate the fact that the two of you have been chummy-chummy of late, which of course is a factor which ought to stand you in good stead. In fact I could go as far as to suggest that is one of the reasons why Greta has refused to help out for the poor misguided creature actually believed your kindly disposition extended towards her and not towards the English Trollope!"

"And why are you so certain that I am willing to persuade her?"

"Oh you will do that all right because if you don't then maybe she will find out exactly who it was that floored Callum Rothwell back in my home port!"

Brett swallowed hard on these words. Nevertheless he was quick to retaliate. "Well if you happen to be around at the time then I can assure you that she most definitely will not consider it!"

"I have already told you that it is my boss who needs the assistance and not I for if it had been me needing assistance then Greta I am sure would most definitely have obliged and consequently I wouldn't be here having to trouble you at this moment!"

"By that one could suppose that Greta has already had some altercation with your boss! Tell me something however, it's just a thought really, but is Callum Rothwell going to be there?"

"Such interest in Callum Rothwell is hardly on the agenda I would have said. But as a subsidiary to his boss I would say yes to your query. I expect that he will be there, in a similar capacity as I will be attending on the day of the agenda!"

"But I thought you said that you wouldn't be around?"

"I shall have no contact with the girl if that is what you are worried about. Still I believe you will come around to my way of thinking when you have had a chance to ponder on the matter. And as for persuading the girl, why that should prove to be quite easy for you considering that you are holding her passport!"

"You seem to know an awful lot!"

"I feel that it is my bent in life to know an awful lot but on the other hand little boys often enjoy the opportunity to split on their elder sister and I must say that I found Steven most enlightening to talk to, that was of course until Rothwell stuck his oar in and had the lad sent back to England which finished any such conversations. Still I suppose the lad had served his purpose by that time especially after broadcasting his feat of imagination almost as if he was hoping that the entire world would hear!" The man gave a coarse laugh as he remembered back to the look of astonishment on the faces of some of his colleagues. "But enough of this frivolity, my boss is due to arrive in the country tomorrow and therefore I expect you to bring the girl round to the centre to meet him, perhaps you could make it some little time before the general assembly takes place with the ritualistic family photograph!" Having imparted his speech Capello made ready to leave. "Just do not fail me my friend otherwise the powers that be may be learning something that will prove to your detriment!"

Brett watched his retreating figure with a sigh for although it might well be jarring against his better judgement to act as directed; this however was something that he had to do if he wanted to keep his own position. The trouble was however getting Rachel to agree. After the previous night he most certainly did not want to relinquish her passport that was for certain, for to have done so would have only succeeded in allowing her to return to England and he did not want that to happen. Therefore it was a rather sombre Brett who showered and dressed that morning as he mused on how on earth he could persuade the girl to act in this manner.

"The answer is a most definite no!" The girl could not have sounded more positive in her refusal. "If Capello wants a stenographer to assist his superior then he will just have to persuade Greta to do the job!" She shuddered at the thought of being anywhere near the Portuguese man even if she was supposedly working for his boss. Of course she had heard about this summit for Callum had mentioned it and she wondered what the expression would be on his face if she turned up taking notes for the Portuguese delegation. Anyway she was not a stenographer; Callum had put it out that way yes, but that had only been for his convenience. She was first and foremost an economist and Brett had to recognise this. For the life of her she felt she could no longer understand this man whom last night had proved to be more endearing to her than she had felt any time before! Moreover he knew full well what she thought of Capello and of that female creep he usually had by his side, therefore why had he decided to ask her in the first place she could not possibly guess?

"Then perhaps you could reconsider. If you do then you will get me out of a jam and I did think that we were friends if nothing more. That is what friends are supposed to do aren't they? Help each other out when the need arises!"

"Then if you claim friendship with me then you should never have asked me in the first place for you know full well my feelings when it is anything to do with that man. If it is so important and Greta is unavailable then I am afraid you will have to find someone else!"

"Then it is not even worth the return of your passport?" Brett had not wanted to say this for by this time he most definitely wanted to keep Rachel for himself but now under the circumstances he felt that he had little alternative.

"So that is your price, is it? And to think after last night I had even begun to forget about the wretched thing!"

"I am afraid that under the circumstances it is my price! I'm sorry Rachel but there is little else that I can do!"

"Maybe having my passport restored and being able to return to England and pursue my own career might be an answer to all our problems!"

"And if I said that I didn't really want you to return back there?"

"Sorry Brett but I thought you suggested that we made a bargain. I will carry out the wretched role of playing the stenographer, much against my better judgement I must say, and in return you will return my passport. At least that way I can possibly look forward to a more peaceful existence back at home than what I can here. For in this place I have rapidly come to the conclusion that you cannot trust anybody's word. I'm not at all surprised that the British people have finally shown some sense and want us out of this mass of intrigue which only serves to cost lots of money!" Her expression now said it all for once again Rachel felt she had been badly let down by the ones she had learned to trust.

"The first minister from Portugal arrives tomorrow the day before the summit is due to take place and therefore I will take you along to his chambers and introduce you!"

"I shall look forward to that like some milk that has turned sour. Perhaps that is a fair enough description to fit the lot of you. Before I go to see this man however I expect to be provided with my flight tickets back to London for the day following this summit, because if they are not in my hands along with my passport on the same day as this summit then you can forget all about me taking part. And now if I have made myself clear you can get out of here Brett for it would only serve to ruin my ethos to have any more to do with you people than what is absolutely necessary!"

Brett scowled but nevertheless he realised that the girl was speaking the truth even if what she had said did not entirely suit his purpose, and now, he decided, the time was not opportune to argue with her. "Very well then if that is the way you want it so be it!" He left hoping against hope that she would call him back but at the same time he realised that would be the easy way out for him. Under the circumstances he would just have to put his brains to work and think up something else!

Maybe the first minister of Portugal was surprised when he found an English girl was to stand in as his stenographer, but at their introduction the man was charm itself even if he silently vowed that he would take Capello to one side and ask him what was going on for as far as he knew that man already had a perfectly good stenographer, well at least if the fee she demanded from his government to carry out this task was anything to go by. But Capello had sworn that Greta was feeling a little under the weather at the time and the girl that he had brought to these chambers had previously acted in support of Callum Rothwell at some other meetings in the past.

"Now is that a fact?" The minister still looked a little dubious as he turned in Rachel's direction. "In that case my dear perhaps you would not mind if I dictated tomorrow's agenda to you and then you can provide me with a copy!"

Rachel pulled a face for she was not so naïve that she did not realise that she was being tested out. But by this time Brett had managed to disappear along with his Portuguese friend and therefore she had no axe to bear against this first minister, always providing Brett returned with her flight tickets as they had agreed. Well if he didn't then she would definitely down tools on the morrow and that was the only thing she could promise herself. But today she would oblige and complete the job that the man had requested.

Perhaps the first minister was quietly pleased with the work that Rachel turned out for him once it was duly typed and printed out. Indeed as she glanced through the final draft Rachel was a perfectionist in requesting him to clarify certain points that he had made which she felt were a little inconclusive. At least he shook her hands warmly as they finished and exerted a promise from her that she would not let him down the following day.

"Are you referring to before or after the family photograph?" She found the quip was something she could not avoid but the minister obviously appreciated her sense of humour for he laughed gustily at her rejoinder.

"I think that it is a great pity that I have promised to be with some very boring friends tonight otherwise my dear I think I would have enjoyed your company in the town, but then my dear no doubt you have friends of your own who will be waiting to see you!"

Rachel smiled but did not respond. After all she could hardly confess to the man that she was far more concerned about getting hold of her passport and her flight ticket back to the U.K than in entertaining any so called friends.

She had not left the building however before she ran unexpectedly into Adri and Dimitri who naturally wanted to make a fuss of her. "We have just had a meeting with the minister from Hungary. He appeared to be very supportive of our submission; in fact he did say that the British minister had been in touch with him on our behalf. So that seems good do you not think? But tell us please why you are here for we did not expect you to be in such a place!"

"I guess I was just trying to oblige a friend!" Rachel responded with a sickly smile before she heard the cough that disturbed then and turning her head saw Capello standing there and upon the sight of that man Rachel visibly shivered.

"Is that so?" Adri sounded unconvinced.

Before she had the chance to respond it was the Portuguese man who spoke. "As a matter of fact the girl is doing me a favour by acting a stenographer to my first minister tomorrow!" Capello uncharacteristically now sounded all sweetness and light as he attempted to explain his presence on the scene.

"Is that so?" Adri repeated whilst at the same time he looked quite unconvinced with the other man's explanation. "But I understood that you already had a good stenographer of your own?"

"Ah you are meaning Greta. I am afraid that at the moment the girl is unwell and therefore unable to attend!"

"That is strange. I was convinced that I saw her when we came into the building!"

"I am afraid you must be mistaken Sir!" Capello may have applied a persuasive tongue but Adri still did not appear to be totally convinced. That was when Capello turned his attention onto Rachel turning away from the two Croatians and dismissing them almost as useless flotsam. "I believe my minister was delighted with your work. I must thank you for getting me out of a jam!"

By this time he had followed her to the lift and it was when they reached ground level that Rachel caught her first glimpse of Greta and she remembered what Adri had said. In fact to her mind the girl did not look ill at all, merely as if she was in some sort of blazing temper and when her eyes rested on Rachel the latter knew exactly who this temper was aimed at.

"So little Miss Prudence now thinks that she will help herself to my job does she? One has to certainly watch out when the English rose shows her petals especially when one considers that she was unable to keep her own man!"

"I understood that you were either unwell or you didn't want to take this job Greta, otherwise you can rest assured that I would not be here for I most certainly do not wish to deprive you of socialising with your so-called elite!"

"So that is what they told you, that I was unwell, is it? How gullible can one get? Pablo merely wished to act like some pawn who was dancing attendance to his master's wishes and he actually thought that I would do his bidding without the mention of any recompense. Why he acted in this manner is something that I do not know and therefore if it is anything that I do not know then I most definitely do not support it and Pablo or anyone else for that matter can think again about what they have asked! Perhaps if I am permitted to make a suggestion, you should also think about matters in this way instead of adopting your usual form of trying to turn from one man to another in your misery!"

Rachel clenched her knuckles tightly. Maybe she was afraid that they could take it upon themselves to lurch out at the speaker for the words of derision that the woman had uttered. But then Greta, being the person whom she was, had decided that any audience with Rachel was now over and done with for she had no intention of giving any more time to this person whom she considered to be a lesser being. Besides she remembered an appointment she had made with the manicurist and that person would be most upset if she broke one of her long finger nails, which after her blonde tresses were her pride and joy. Therefore she consequently turned and left the other girl to simmer in her anger and decided that being able to observe such anger spreading to the face of Rachel Burton was well worth her effort!

Rachel tried her best to content herself with the knowledge that Brett was now due to keep his promise for she had completed the first part of the bargain and therefore she poised herself to wait in the foyer for his return. It would be good to shake the dust from this place off her feet and get back to England with her mundane job alongside of Eric Taylor. Now the knowledge of whether she had passed her first step towards her articles didn't seem to matter anymore for all she wanted to do was to get back to some form of sanity even if this meant she had to study for her board yet again.

At least such thoughts of England were pleasant until she realised that the time had slipped by without Brett's appearance and as she began to shuffle a little in her shoes another voice assailed her. "I can't say that I was totally surprised to spot you here today although I must say the company you keep is enough to make any upstanding male want to pewk!" She turned on her heels to see Callum eyeing her with a mixture of disbelief and disgust upon his face. "Funny really but when we were together on that cruise I never imagined you could be so two faced!"

"In that case Mr Rothwell what gives you the idea that you have any room to talk especially when one considers your penchant for collecting women whilst on your travels?"

"What the hell are you talking about now woman?"

"Perhaps it would be more appropriate if you stopped trying to play the Mr Innocent with me for I have heard that you have a different girl in every place your Superiors decide to send you!"

"That is what you have heard you say, and may I question who imparted such secrets into your delicate lobes?"

"No, you may not question!" Maybe Rachel was almost relieved to see Brett finally approaching, but his arrival seemed to do little for Callum, for making a laudable oath at the sight of that man Callum decided it was time for him to leave.

"Catching up on old times then?" Brett had a sneer-like quality in his voice as he realised whom she had been speaking to.

"No I have not. I was merely waiting here for you!"

"And there was I believing that you were entertaining an old flame! Tell me however how did your meeting with the minister go?"

"It passed all right. Now have you brought my flight ticket as you promised you would do: I believe that was your side of the bargain if I remember correctly?"

"Your blasted flight ticket for the day after tomorrow is here!" Brett fished in his pocket to produce an envelope, which after handing it to Rachel she tore open to make sure the contents were within. "Satisfied then that I have kept my part of the bargain?"

"And where exactly is my passport for these tickets are useless without it?"

"I don't remember that was a part of the bargain and in any case I would not dream of relinquishing that until after the summit is over. Before that time I might seek the opportunity to persuade you to change your mind!"

"That is something that you have no chance of succeeding in doing. I have already promised to do your dirty work for you therefore as far as I am concerned you can go to hell!"

"I'm afraid that you will have to be nicer to me than that if you want to see your passport again!"

"Don't worry for if necessary I will go to the British Embassy!"

"By the time you have completed that mission your plane will have well and truly left. If you are therefore serious about getting back to your provincial hum drum occupation then you will have to try to be a little pleasanter. And that is a task that you can start on tonight! Have I made myself clear?"

"Perfectly clear but I promise you now you will get no satisfaction from me!"

"Perhaps we will wait and see on that score. I will pick you up at your apartment at seven thirty tonight!"

"The janitor objects to one receiving masculine callers during the hours of darkness!"

"Does he now? I didn't think he raised any objections before. But if he is of that mind then perhaps we had better try to change it for him!"

Rachel fumed. She now had no intention of allowing him to escort her anywhere. Her apartment was not far distance but first she resolved to visit a local snack bar to grab a spot of lunch and that was something she intended to do on her own: After that she would make absolutely sure that she was well away from the premises well before seven that evening. In the meantime her task was to get well away from this man for there was no way she intended him to follow her, therefore after making an excuse to visit the ladies she made her escape by exiting the place through another door.

Even so if Rachel intended to remain solo for the rest of the day then she was doomed to be disappointed. For no sooner had she arrived back at the apartment after finishing her snack and vowing to herself that she would not answer any calls made on her for the rest of the day that she spotted a certain figure waiting for her in the foyer and there was certainly no means of escape from this individual.

"I require a little peace therefore what the hell are you doing here? I imagined by your tone and the way you said I made you feel sick that you would be the last person to turn up begging on my doorstep!"

"Believe you me I am not begging for now I am distinctly telling you that you are going straight back to England!"

"And why should I want to listen to you. I am returning to England as a matter of fact but not until after the summit meeting for I have been employed to complete a task there!"

"You will leave before the summit. It is far too damned dangerous here for you to stay around any longer!"

"And if I say that I am not leaving then who do you think you are to make me, apart that is from the fact that you are a male chauvinistic prig!"

"Fortunately for you it was Adri who managed to inform me who you were working for much to his credit. That was when I decided that I had to do something about it. Anyway I believe you wanted to know who it was who knocked me out in Lisbon therefore if you still require an answer why not question your so-called friend about the matter and then tell me that I am behaving like a male chauvinist!"

"But why should I? After all I know full well who it was that accosted you" Maybe her mouth had now sagged open in surprise and she was rewarded with a rueful smile from the one she had verbally accosted.

"You actually thought that it was Pablo didn't you?" He gave a harsh laugh. "Well one must admit that whilst person is not beyond carrying out such an action, this time around the blame cannot be laid on his shoulders!"

"Then who was it then?"

"If you really want an answer to your question then perhaps you would do better to start and look a little closer to home!"

"You are referring to Brett I suppose. That is complete nonsense for why should he seek to do such a thing?"

"I suggest that he received his instructions from his masters and you know full well who they are!"

"That is total rubbish. After all Brett is a member of the I.M.F.!"

"The man is a double dealer. Not that I expect you to understand a great deal about such people!"

"You speak now of a double dealer? Are you meaning something like a man who has a different woman at every port of call?"

"So I presume that is what he told you and you believed him. To think I actually thought that I had found someone special in you. But there again would you believe me if I assured you that there has been no other woman either before or since meeting you?"

"Quite frankly I don't know what to believe or who to trust anymore!"

"And to think that I was once under the mistaken allusion that you trusted me!"

"If I remember correctly you never attempted to contact me to say where you where and what had happened to you!"

"Perhaps you expected my response a little too early. Perhaps it never occurred to you that I wanted to protect you until this business was over. Your itchy fingers seemed to be determined to get into the action and therefore you sought your solace in the wrong quarter. Now I can only advise you to take those same fingers back again to England before they get burnt!"

"Sorry but I cannot go because as I previously stated I have promised to do a job here in this place. So if that is all you have to say Mr Rothwell perhaps you should think of leaving right now for I have a busy schedule in front of me!" It hurt her to have to issue such words but so far she had not got her passport back and she could not expect to receive it until she had carried out certain commitments.

"Then if you have made up your mind I suppose there is little else that one can say to you!" Callum had somewhat reluctantly drawn himself up to his full height. "I guess I won't be troubling you again, I can only pray that good fortune befalls you!"

She knew he was in the process of leaving and with all of her heart she now wanted to call him back if only to explain that she couldn't return to England at the time, not until she completed the chore set for her and had her passport returned, but then, she reminded herself, if she admitted that it was Brett who was holding on to this as some form of blackmail she dreaded the consequences, more indeed for Callum's sake especially if the complete trio turned on him if he tried to retrieve it for her. It was far better this way for Callum's work she admitted was of National importance and as such nothing should be allowed to impede upon it. Therefore she watched him go, the tears of frustration now turning into those of sorrow. Maybe one day the opportunity would arise for her to explain to him why she had turned him away; that was providing he would listen for there was no doubt left in her mind that she still loved him and his own explanation of what had happened in the past had now sufficed to quell any lingering doubts!

Even so she still had to face the prospect of getting hold of that damned passport if Brett did not keep his word and relinquish it after the summit meeting on the following day, but she had the night to puzzle that one out. Once inside of her apartment with the door locked behind her for come what may she was still determined that she would not go out with Brett that evening, especially now she had learnt the name of the person who actually floored Callum back in Lisbon, Rachel took a look at the flight time on the air ticket. It maintained that she had to check in no later than eighteen thirty the next day and Rachel bit her lip for this did not afford her very much time to secure the documentation after the summit had finished. But somehow secure it she would, she promised herself as she hastily changed into casual gear, rinsed her face, drew a comb through her mop and then got ready to leave the apartment before Brett came anywhere near!

Of course she knew that he was annoyed at having been stood up when she saw him the following morning, but Rachel had gone to the conference hall in order to do a job of work and at the time she had a good excuse for not speaking to him apart that was from a cursory good morning in his direction. Perhaps it was indeed fortunate that he was not able to follow her into that place, the only trouble being that Pablo was there and what was more the man from Portugal intended to let her know that he was aware that she had stood Brett up.

"So what happened last night then for I believe you stood my friend up? I don't think he is very pleased about it either. If a woman ever dared to do that to me then she would certainly feel the consequences!"

"If you must know I was tired and I had a headache through all that typing yesterday. I left a message with the janitor that I was not to be disturbed!"

"That seems to be a likely story! Of course it wouldn't have anything to do with Callum Rothwell following you back to your apartment would it?"

"No, if you must know Callum tried to persuade me to return to England yesterday and to forgo this conference. Well he didn't have very much luck did he, considering that I am now here and ready to act as stenographer to your superior this morning? Therefore perhaps you can inform your so-called friend of that for just at this moment I am afraid that I cannot spare the time!"

Pablo watched her as she made her way to the lift and a different expression suddenly gilded his eyes. Perhaps indeed he was now seeing Rachel in a new light and someone he could possibly have a use for in the future, but his thoughts were disturbed with the advent of Greta, who after following the direction his eyes had taken, grabbed hold of Pablo by the arm with a series of remonstrations. Thus the man from Portugal had to be content to be persuaded to walk away even as Greta herself cast an eye of impending doom over the retreating girl.

That being said Rachel's role at the conference appeared to go very well. As most of the discussion was held in English she needed no translation of the speech, which proved to be some relief to her, and she could tell from the comments that were passed afterwards that her mentor's contribution was also well received.

"And that, if I may say so, is all your doing. Maybe you are looking for some more permanent employment Miss Burton?" He looked hopeful in her direction but Rachel shook her head.

"I am sorry but I am afraid that I am already spoken for. You see I have a job back in England that I am now anxious to get back to!"

"So who do you act as stenographer for back in England?"

"I am not a stenographer Sir; actually I am an economist working for a chartered accountant and trying desperately to find the time to take my articles!"

"Maybe you should consider that you could be wasting your time?" Rachel shook her head with a smile. "In that case I think that your employer is a very lucky man. But take my card and if you do change your mind then please get in touch with me for I do not like to see such talent as your own going to waste!" He handed her a business card before continuing. "There is also a cheque for you that I have left with my aide, Pablo Capello, of course you know the man don't you? A little bit of the hard diamond I would say but very necessary to me in my line of work!"

Even so the smile that she left the minister with soon faded when Rachel espied the trio who were awaiting her return in the reception of the place. Pablo had a rather cynical expression on his face but nevertheless handed her the packet containing the cheque as payment for her services. "My minister obviously considered that you were worth every penny of this for your services!" The tone of his voice was not what one could consider to be pleasant. Indeed one was left with the impression that the sting was shortly to follow. And maybe that came as she turned her attention to Brett who by this time had Greta clinging to his arm and making sympathetic noises in his ear.

"I think that you promised to hand me my passport back!" Rachel appeared unperturbed but that feeling was only on the surface, for already she had begun to feel something of the aura that was to follow.

"It is still at my apartment. You will have to come with me in order to get it!" Rachel glanced at her watch, the time was passing she really had little time to spare.

"Why should you give it to her just because she asked?" It was Greta once again casting a supercilious glance in her direction.

"I did promise!" From his expression Rachel could not gauge whether Brett meant the words or not.

"But why should she give you the run around. Let her miss her damned flight, perhaps you could even assign her to me and I will teach her some manners!" The woman pouted in Brett's direction, not behaving as if she was asking a favour but rather something that she was expecting.

"I'm afraid that I have need of you Greta!" It was Pablo who spoke. "Nice try I must admit but I think it is up to Brett to decide what he is going to do about the matter!" He took the girl by the arm much to the others disgust for she obviously objected to being removed from a scene where she felt she could add her two penny worth.

"I have already said that I will see to the matter!" This time it was Brett who added fuel to Pablo's argument. "I think I said that your passport is at my apartment Rachel. Therefore if you want it in order to catch your plane then we had better go for it now!"

Rachel was sure that it was Pablo who held Greta back as they finally left, Rachel again reminding herself of the time as the minutes appeared to simply fly by. She had already packed her case so she supposed that was one blessing. Indeed her first thought had been to return all her clothes back to Brett for he was the one who had purchased most of them in the first place, but then sanity prevailed for after all she could hardly return to England wearing nothing but some loose ill-fitting clothing and without even a jersey or a coat, especially after listening to the weather forecast with snow ice and a bitterly cold wind hitting those Northern shores.

Arriving back Brett made no bones about retrieving the passport and holding it out for her to see. Initially she went to grab it, anxious now to be getting away from the lot of them.

"Not yet!" And with that he placed the passport on a top shelf where it was obvious for all to see. "First I want to know just how much you want this documentation!"

"But you know full well that I do. We made a bargain remember!"

"That was before you stood me up last night. Now you will have to prove to me just how much you do want it. My price is high so exactly what are you prepared to do in order to get hold of the blasted thing!"

"You have no right to hold on to my property!"

"I believe that I have every right. My question to you was what are you prepared to do in order to win it back?" Rachel automatically glanced at her watch only to draw a caustic smile from her companion. "You are quite right, the time is getting on therefore you have little time to make your decision, that is always providing that you want to catch your plane!"

By now Rachel decided that there was little point in arguing with the man. Instead she slipped off her coat whilst at the same time plotting how she could get her hands on the damned document. "Ah now you are beginning to get the idea, but you will have to take more off than your coat. The fact is that I want you Rachel and what is more I am fully determined to get my wishes.

Therefore at the risk of repeating myself, you have not got much time to make it good!"

"I need the bathroom!" It was a lamentable excuse but it was enough to get her away from the main action if only on a temporary basis.

"Then don't take all day about it, remember the clock is ticking!"

Once she was inside of the place Rachel locked the door and then leant against it. Already she was beginning to realise that Brett had no intention of giving her back her passport even if she acceded to his wishes, which she certainly had no intention of doing. It was whilst she was still pondering on her next move that she heard another door in the flat open and she realised that Brett must have left the main area.

It was then that she acted quickly and thanked her lucky stars that she had been good at netball at school. At least they had told her she was an excellent shooter. Without thinking any further about it and trying her best not to worry that Brett would hear her and return, she was back in the room as quick as a flash. A chair helped her to balance in order to reach the blasted object but once she had it in her hand then she was away from the place as fast as her legs could carry her without caring whether Brett had heard her or even followed her just so long as he did not catch up with her.

Perhaps she was fortunate that a taxi was passing by at that time and he was looking for a fare, therefore in some ways the rest was simple. Her case was already packed and the taxi driver was willing to wait whilst she raced into the apartment block to collect it. After that it was full speed in the direction of the airport clutching both her flight ticket and her passport in her hand.

Perhaps the airport authorities believed that they had one eccentric woman on their hands, a person who was constantly looking over her shoulder as if she was expecting someone to follow her and snatch her away, but finally she had her boarding card issued and Rachel was well on her way to the departure lounge. It was only when she reached this place that she permitted herself to relax for no one without a boarding card could enter this area and besides the plane was already signposted indicating that one should now proceed to the gate ready for boarding.

⋆ ⋆ ⋆ ⋆

Chapter Eleven

Perhaps Rachel was still feeling a little jumpy after this experience when she arrived at the airport, yet she managed to pass through the security checks quite easily. Still the fact that a person came to sit next to her whilst they were waiting to board at the gate startled her, especially when, after glancing across at this figure with some fear and trepidation, she realised that the one sitting close to her was Callum.

"Sorry if I startled you but rest assured I am not following you!" His voice, once he realised she had noticed him, sounded rather caustic as he motioned around the area to indicate that there was nowhere else left for him to sit and more or less intimated that had there been somewhere else then he wouldn't be sitting next to her. "My Superior has now finished his task at the summit and therefore it is time for me to report back again to London. I'm afraid that the minions, like me, have to travel back third class, unlike our Lords and Masters!"

Rachel gulped for at the time words seemed to have deserted her. Not that Callum appeared to welcome any conversation from her at this stage. For a moment she wondered whether they would be sitting together on the plane and she even allowed herself to day dream a little. Yet after looking at his demeanour she decided that Callum would not be at all pleased if that turned out to be a fact. Glancing now at her boarding card she remonstrated with herself for deeming to act in such a ridiculous manner. Anyway, she argued with herself, why should she want to be sat next to a man who had, for reasons of his own, somehow destroyed the very emotion she had once felt for him? Or had that emotion really been destroyed for as far as she was concerned just sensing his presence there had sent her pulses racing?

In the event however when they boarded the plane they were finally seated many rows apart from each other although much to her dismay her stupid heart had to give her away with panging its remorse like a church bell sounds in mourning. Maybe, she decided, if they had been sat closer together she could have managed to discover why he had never contacted her after his accident despite her repeated pleas. But it now seemed as if fate had definitely shown its hand and in all truth Callum seemed much to prefer staring into his newspaper then even to spare a glance in her direction and once again the pangs of knowing full well that she was supposed to forget all about him hit her like a cold shower.

The flight was not a long one in it duration and yet it seemed to take many hours to Rachel before they finally touched down at Gatwick. Hours that were spent wondering what life would have been like with Callum by her side and cursing the day when their relationship had apparently drawn to a close. At Gatwick too the same momentum was to be repeated for Callum's luggage appeared quite quickly on that conveyor belt unlike her own, and after rescuing it he quickly disappeared without even casting a glance in her direction. It now seemed blatantly obvious that he still believed that she had sold out to the opposing forces and once Callum believed anything like that then he blatantly refused to have anything to do with anyone who answered this description.

Thus it was a sad and wiser Rachel who finally made her way to Euston station in order to catch the train that was travelling back to the Northern parts of the country, each mile now serving to remind her that it was taking her and further away from the man she still loved as the train relentlessly beat out its rhythm along the track. She had taken the time to ring Eric Taylor before she had left Euston for by this time she almost believed her infamy must have spread far and wide and no one would want to know her. Still Eric went some way in trying to cheer her by saying that he was relieved to know she was back in the country and yes he would be expecting her to report back to the office the following morning.

"Because by my reckoning you have had a long enough holiday and there is also a mound of work piling up on your desk. Enough that is to keep you busy and to stop you thinking of downing tools again to go off simply anywhere when somebody snaps their fingers!"

Rachel knew Eric Taylor well enough to know that he was gesturing and during the journey back to the North of the country she tried to occupy herself by attempting to guess the reasons why other passengers had seen fit to travel that day. Nevertheless this in itself did not suffice enough to occupy her mind fully and the constant memory of what had transpired of late and especially Callum's attitude towards her kept rearing its ugly head, so much so that she was relieved when the train finally drew into Manchester station and she could actively do something even if this was only to stretch her legs!

It was too late to see anyone on the day she arrived back and yet all the promises she made to herself of getting a good night's sleep failed to refresh her and consequently the following morning she returned to her former place of work looking rather tired and a little red around the eyes. Perhaps it was rather unfortunate that the first person she was to clap her eyes on was that dratted boy from the office, Ian, who it appeared had been waiting for her and was obviously more than a little determined to add to her misery.

"Sorry about your articles Rachel. But never mind I suppose you will be able to take them again next year. I passed my exams so I suppose that now places me on the same level as what you are in the workplace. That seems to be a little strange because up until now I have always been your junior but now we are both of equal status!"

Perhaps it was fortunate that Eric, with his usual habit of punctuality, made his grand entrance at this precise moment otherwise Rachel did not know how she would have responded, but seeing Rachel standing there in an obviously distraught manner, Eric immediately read into the situation and motioned her to come into his office.

"Please don't let the lad worry you child. As a matter of fact he has been having things all his own way for far too long around here, so it will be good to have you back in order to keep him in check! But then in all honesty I don't really think that really is what is troubling you. What is the matter Rachel, and please don't fib to me for I have known you for far too long to allow you to get away with any such fabrications?"

"I seem to have made rather a hash of things!" Talk was the last thing that Rachel wanted to do and yet she knew full well that Eric would not be content until he was satisfied that he knew the reason for her morose state.

"Perhaps you had better sit yourself down right there and tell me all then!"

Rachel forced a winsome smile onto her face as she did as he requested knowing full well that she would not escape from this room until she had told Eric the whole story.

"I see!" The man nodded as she finally paused for breath. Relating all that had happened did appear to have given her some relief surprisingly enough for she knew that Eric was a person whom one could trust in. "So what you are actually telling me is that you managed to find Callum again but then lost him in the face of this Brett Chaplain and his associates?"

"I suppose so if you put it like that!"

"I don't suppose you have seen the television news this morning?" She shook her head now wondering what the man had in mind for watching the television at that time of the day was certainly something Rachel did not subscribe to.

"It was under breaking news actually with little other detail apart from the fact that an Englishman by the name of Brett Chaplain has been arrested in Brussels: Something to do with an incident in a pub last night with another man and a girl!"

"I can imagine who they were. I guess one side of me is sorry that it had to happen but the other side of me could hardly care less!"

"Well at least the fellow who was bearing that title can hardly follow you here now so that is one thing to be thankful for. But I believe that you said Callum had now come back to London?"

"Callum and I are finished, he made that perfectly clear. Well you have had the whole story now Eric so perhaps it is time I got to work on all of those papers you mentioned that had been left on my desk!"

"Ah yes ---well-------!"

"Please don't tell me that Ian has seen to them!"

"Only some of the more immediate ones, he is partially qualified now you know!"

"Yes I know, he past his exams and is now on the same level as myself, that is what he told me, and I also believe that I made a dismal impression on the board!"

"In actual fact you made quite a good impression on the board. It was just that they felt you needed time to sort yourself out a little more and therefore they have asked for a review in six months' time, which is far better than having to wait for a full year!"

"In that case perhaps I had better start my work as soon as possible!" She stood to leave. Eric was a kindly soul and she supposed very much in the fatherly position but there were certain matters she had to see to for herself.

"Very well then have it your way. But if there is anything else that is still troubling you please come back and see me. Personally I prefer to see you smiling like you used to do rather than looking so morose and sad!"

"I promise I will do my best, for after all I suppose what happened in the past is now well and truly over with!" She forced a half smile on her face, which almost appeared to have been painted there as she made her leave whilst once back again in the main office Ian, for good measure, cackled something about her still being teacher's pet as she made for her desk.

In truth she soon found that the pile of work that Eric had intimated was waiting for her had been dwindled down to simply two or three sheets of non-important items that she spent the whole morning toying with rather than desiring to appear idle on her first morning back whilst Ian appeared to spend the whole of the time rushing backwards and forwards to the boss' office with papers in his hand leaving her to feel very much the office junior and quite an ineffective one at that.

It was on the third day that the flowers arrived via 'Interflora' with a card attached to them that was addressed to her. She saw the eyebrows in that office slightly raised as she detached the card from off the wrappings, an envelope upon which was scribed one solitary word, simply 'Sorry' and now more than a little curious, Rachel tore it open. Perhaps in her heart she had hoped that the flowers had come from someone else, a person that even now she never stopped thinking about. A silly dream really for why would the man now decide to send her flowers when he had made it perfectly clear that their relationship was well and truly over. Thus quelling the tears that threatened even then to spill over onto her cheeks she began to read the note inside whilst her audience at the time were left to speculate on who the sender of these flowers could be.

The note as well as the flowers, as it turned out, had come from her brother Steven, expressing regret for the way he had behaved, yet one sentence of the hastily scribbled paper once again served to tear at her heart strings. "I have joined the army now. Guess that bloke of yours Callum is some guy for fixing it up for me after the way I behaved. Anyway off for training on Dartmoor for a spell. Guess that should be good. Sorry again for the trouble I caused: But here's wishing you and Callum every happiness---------Steve."

Every happiness! That was a laugh and one that caused the tears in her eyes to well even further! It was Eric who noticed the tears on her face as he passed her by and the man frowned. For one thing he didn't like to see this girl behaving in this manner. He did not like to see her upset and to his mind it was ever since she had been in contact with Callum Rothwell that this change had come over her. Thus Eric Taylor retreated back to his own sac recant quite determined as to what he should do. He glanced at a leaflet on his desk, an advertisement that had recently been placed there, and then murmured something about 'this should do' before he picked up the telephone and nodded his head as if a thought had just occurred to him.

"Guess you know who this is John! ------Yes, you're right as usual. --------- And the top of the morning to you as well. -------And how is business? ------ But this is not really a social call apart from it is good to hear your voice again: Tell me something, this forthcoming exhibition at Birmingham is your firm featured there? ------They are? ----- That's good because I was thinking of bringing a colleague of mine down to cost some of the equipment we would need for our office ------- What do you mean when you ask why a firm of accountants should need exercise stuff. ------Never mind the innuendo of sitting around on our backsides every day, haven't you heard about the de-stressing notion that is currently being bandied about? Well it appears that I have a kid here who needs distressing as of yesterday! Tell me what Stand will you be on for I don't fancy wandering around that exhibition centre all day looking for you? ---------Stand Thirty Four you say? Well I will see you there say on Friday, make it around noon to give us a chance with all the traffic. ------O.K. I will look forward to seeing you again John!" Eric Taylor smiled as he put down the receiver. That was one phone call done and now for the other. Having discovered that such a venue was taking place and that his contact would be there he now had no hesitation in picking up the receiver for a second time.

"Hi---Callum, --------- Yes you are right. How are you boy, guess I haven't seen you for a while?------- No, this is not strictly business but a little bird told me that you were due for a spot of leave and I wondered if you had read about the exhibition coming up in Birmingham next weekend? Thought it would be right up your street considering your hobby of extreme sports. --------What do you mean, of course I remember? Let's face it you used to frighten the life out of us with your antics whilst you were still at college. Anyway I believe they are erecting a climbing wall there so you will be able to check whether your prowess has slipped over the years. -------- Why am I telling you all this? Oh you of a suspicious nature. Well if you must know I have one girl here who has never been the same since she met you and what is more I am paying her wages for being moped. That is one thing I don't like, paying to have someone casting misery over the whole office!----- I don't pretend to know what went on between you but I think it is time the pair of you sorted it out once and for all. -------- What do you mean it is finished? -------Well I have a girl here who doesn't want to think so -----------Brett Chaplain did you say? The last thing I knew about Brett Chaplain before his arrest, according to the latest news, was that she had been trying to avoid the fellow like the plague although I do know he made her act as stenographer to that man from Portugal before he gave her passport back. And from all reports she did a damned good job there. In fact I'm dreading the Portuguese boss chap getting in touch with me and wanting to use her again. So my advice to you as your former tutor and mentor is to make sure that you are at the exhibition centre round about noon on Friday --------- No the girl doesn't know a damned thing about this, nor am I likely to tell her! I've taken it upon myself to ring you otherwise I know full well she would refuse to come with me to cost up some equipment, that is the reason I shall give her when I tell her she is coming. --------- Now just don't let me down! --------What do you mean it is up to Rachel? I thought that you were the man in this relationship, so do something about it before I run out of tissues!"

Ringing off Eric Taylor afforded himself a smile. At least he felt a little more satisfied now that he had set the ball in motion. To his mind persuading Rachel would be no trouble at all. Especially if she was led to believe that such activities such as costing up certain de-stressing material for office use would look well on the report that had to be submitted to the board on her behalf!

He waited until the afternoon before he called her into the office for such deliberations required a satisfying lunch whilst he could muse over what he intended to say and once she was called into his sanctum Rachel came along feeling puzzled as to what she had now done wrong.

"Take a look at this!" Eric promptly handed over the leaflet whilst he studied her puzzled expression, his role in all of this now providing at least some amusement for him. "I presume that you have heard of the new notion of exercise for de-stressing employees in the workplace?"

Rachel still looked puzzled. Of course she had heard of such things employed by the multi-nationals but surely they were a different case to their own. For starters where on earth would they place any such apparatus for they had hardly any space for that sort of equipment here in the office? Perhaps Eric read her thoughts. "I know what you are thinking girl but in case you are interested I have got an option on renting the place next door. Not a massive place but it could serve us well for a small work out zone. The thing is that we need to keep up to date and apparently this is the thing to do in today's climate if one wants to keep one's workers healthy!"

"Sorry but I had never considered that factor before. But tell me how does this affect me?"

"There is an exhibition due this weekend at Birmingham. I intend to go and I was wondering if you would like to come along?"

"But I have only just come back to work. You can't surely want me to take more time off?"

"Not time off my dear. I appreciate your company that is true but my ulterior motive is that I would like you to come in order to choose and cost up any equipment you see there that could be of some use to us in the future. There is an additional bonus for you as well, for if you take my advice such efforts would be well appreciated by your board for they obviously like to see people showing initiative!"

"So what had you in mind then?" Rachel knew full well that she could not refuse Eric for the man in his turn had been so kind to her. At the same time the mention that such an endeavour would be viewed favourably by the Board at her next interview made this an opportunity she dare not miss!

"I thought we would travel down there on Friday and thus avoid the weekend rush. If we leave here Friday morning we should be there for lunchtime which will allow you several hours in the afternoon to complete your agenda and then we will drive back Friday evening. I will have to be back by eight for the wife has some friends coming round and I will be in trouble if I am late. Anyway I have already phoned a friend of mine down there and John is expecting us around lunchtime so he will be our first port of call!"

"So you intend driving down there yourself?"

"Of course I do. I do happen to still have a driving license you know I am not that decrepit!" Rachel had to smile at his words for nobody would ever describe Eric Taylor as being decrepit. "So I take it that you will come with me?"

"Do you mean to say that I have an option?"

"No, not really: Still I must say that quip out of you is more like the Rachel I once knew. Anyway I promise that I will have you back for Friday evening if you have any engagements on!"

"I'm afraid that I haven't, not anymore!"

"Then cheer up for goodness sake, at least you will have a chance to test out your prowess on Friday and John, the fellow I spoke about is very helpful!"

Rachel nodded still not totally convinced but then this work was expected of her and after all if it counted with her board as Eric had suggested, then it couldn't be totally bad.

"All right what did the boss want with you now?" It was Ian trying to find out what was going on as she left Eric's office and suddenly Rachel felt glad that she could boast that she was going somewhere with the boss if only to irritate the one who served to annoy her.

"Nothing really: Actually he wants me to go to Birmingham with him on Friday to cost up some new equipment that we might possibly be getting!"

"What? Do you mean that I am to be left here to cope on my own?"

"Well you are qualified now Ian as you seem to be at pains to keep reminding me, so there is no reason why you shouldn't be left in charge of things whilst we are away. After all it is only for the day!"

"What's all this about new equipment then? I haven't heard anything about it!"

"That is probably because Eric has only just received the pamphlet about it and he has decided that all the staff need to be de-stressed after working with you!"

"But there is no room here to house any new equipment that is not relevant to office needs!"

"Eric seems to have had that in his mind; in fact he was speaking of renting some more floor space from next door!"

"First I've heard about it!" He moved away from her muttering something that was not over flattering and his action caused Rachel to half smile yet again. Well in all truth, she decided, the bloated bigot deserved something like this!

Eric called for her promptly at eight o'clock the following Friday morning. To Rachel's mind her boss appeared to be a little blasé as they drove down the motorway, almost indeed as if some weight had now been lifted from his mind. Not that he bothered to explain anything except for being his usual courteous self, interspersing the journey with frequent short stops where they could stretch their legs or call for a coffee. He did enquire at one stage whether she had brought her laptop with her so that she could write up an agenda, but as that had been pretty obvious from the start she did wonder why he had stopped to query.

"Well you will probably need it unless you want to write down all the facts and figures by hand!" It was an excuse she knew but one that she was willing to ignore as she settled back to enjoy the drive and try to relax before the trials of this exhibition loomed up in front of her, for at the time she had no idea at all what Eric had in mind for this de-stressing acquisition and come to think of it she did not even know whether the premises next door to their offices were to be vacated by their present tenants. But then such minor details did not appear to worry Eric!

They finally arrived at the exhibition centre just short of noon and Eric then insisted that they should go and call on John first of all before searching for a bite to eat.

"That's because I arranged to see him on the Stand around this time!" At least he provided her with that information. "That way, if you know where the exhibits are placed you will be able to get to work costing and making up some sort of agenda as soon as we have had a spot of lunch!"

The idea sounded feasible enough she had to admit and within a very short time Rachel found herself being introduced to John who in turn greeted Eric with a slap on the back and with the description of being an old dog. It was quite obvious that the two of them were old friends so whilst their greeting took place Rachel turned away to view some of the equipment that was being displayed. What possibly fascinated her most was the presence of one gigantic climbing wall in the place and she was wondering how on earth they had managed to get an object of that size into the exhibition. A smile touched her lips as she then mused on what Eric would have to say if she recommended one of these for the staff to de-stress upon and it was as she regarded the object in some awe that she noticed a figure even now three parts of the way to the top of it.

Whether this was some athlete employed by the exhibition to demonstrate this climbing wall she could only guess as she turned round to draw Eric's attention to the monstrosity. Yet Eric and John appeared to have taken it into their heads now to disappear leaving her in the middle of nowhere and wondering what to do next.

Feeling sure that Eric would make his reappearance shortly if it was only to insist on taking lunch, she turned back once again to watch the athlete who by this time was making his descent, a great deal quicker than when he had climbed up. Once he was at the bottom of the wall the climber made to remove his helmet and harness, and it was Rachel's turn to gasp as she recognised that shock of hair: Hair that she had once run her hands through, hair that she knew the texture of! Moreover the climber, having dispensed with his gear had obviously also spotted her standing there and was now making his way in her direction. Perhaps at this point Rachel would have moved but now her feet suddenly seemed to be firmly anchored to the ground.

"O.K. so we meet again!" He nodded in her direction as he finally reached her side. "But before you say anything I need to tell you that I am here first and foremost not so much for the climbing but rather to see you and apologise for my behaviour. Whilst I know that you have every right to refuse, will you please accept my apology before we start!"

"Before we start what?" Still reeling in shock at seeing him here Rachel did not know how to respond and consequently looked around for reinforcement from Eric but of course the man had not returned.

"What I meant to say before was we start where we left off of course!" And, as if to give emphasis to these words his arms were now out-stretched as they inched their way towards her shoulders. "Don't bother looking for Eric for some little time for I guess he has done a runner with that old friend of his: Conveniently too I would suggest, so that we could be left alone. First however you can begin by telling me why you never let me know that Brett Chaplain was holding onto your passport and blackmailing you?"

"Always supposing it had been possible to contact you at that stage, then what would you have done? Indeed what could you have done apart that is from probably getting yourself knocked out again at the very least!"

"Oh ye of little faith! Is that what you really think of me Rachel? But I think perhaps you had better start at the beginning and tell me what happened!" The arms that had been outstretched were now nestling upon her shoulders as if they were offering some form of comfort and Rachel shuddered in anticipation before she managed to find the voice to continue, for there were still more questions she needed to ask.

"After you disappeared in Portugal I tried to contact you but there was never any reply!"

"And why do you think that was? I was simply trying my best to protect you at the time and then when I turned around you appeared to have aligned yourself with the ones I was trying to protect you from. What was a man supposed to think? In fact it took Eric to put me back on the right track when he described your sorry state and demanded to know my intentions towards you!"

So it had been Eric who had managed to contact him and tell him that they would be coming here today, For a moment she did not know whether to love or hate her boss for interfering, but the look that was now in

Callum's eyes soon persuaded her that perhaps she had a great deal to thank Eric for. But there was still much that was left to say. "You could have tried asking me I suppose. After you had disappeared Brett suddenly appeared to be most supportive, of course I didn't know the reason that lay behind his kindness at the time. But after I had returned to England and partly due to the antics of my own brother, I found myself in the clutches of Greta who seemed determined to prise secrets about you from out of my head and it was Brett who put on the show of rescuing me from her talons insisting that I would be far safer in Brussels than remaining in this country. Like a fool I believed him that was until those colleagues of his arrived on the scene and by that time the return of my passport was my reward for acting as a stenographer to the Portuguese minister at the summit. Whilst I have no regrets for helping that individual out, for the man was a perfect gentleman and wanted to find me a job permanently with his team, I am afraid that I did not get my passport back as promised. That was when I took things into my own hands and well I did see you on the plane coming back to England, but by that time you didn't want to know me!"

"You actually think that I didn't want to know you? Rachel I realise that I have been a complete idiot but perhaps the truth of the matter was that I couldn't bear the thought of losing you to any other man let alone Brett Chaplain. You see I happened to fall in love with you the very first time I met you at that hotel in Manchester. Why else do you suppose I decided to fly out to the boat earlier than expected? I wanted to get to know you better, and the more we were together then the more I found myself captivated under your spell. But now is there any chance that I might be forgiven do you think?"

Perhaps the look in her eyes provided him with the answer he wanted to know for the next moment he drew her close and then apparently completely oblivious to the crowds visiting the exhibition at that time, placed his lips on her own. Immediately she began to feel the tensions which had built up inside of her beginning to melt away and she no longer had any recollection of where she was apart from the fact that she felt safe in his arms.

"They told me that you had a girl in every port as well!" As she came up for air the words came out almost involuntarily.

"And you believed them? Rachel I may work for the Ministry but I am not James Bond. There has only ever been one girl in my life and now she is standing right here besides me. What is more this time around I have no intention of letting her go for I intend marrying her at the first opportunity. As I have some leave pending how do you fancy a honeymoon in the States, I know your sister is there, so we could combine family ties with our holiday?"

"Callum, how on earth can I ask Eric for time off again at the moment?" Again Rachel felt at a loss for words.

"That is some response to my proposal I must say! But if it makes you feel any better, then somehow I am under the impression that Eric does not expect you to be going back to Manchester with him today or anytime soon!"

"But what about the apparatus for de-stressing that I supposed to be costing?"

"In a nutshell I guess any apparatus is me, for it appears that you are the one who needed to be de-stressed and I am the one to see to it, like this!" Once again his lips enfolded hers and this time the situation was not one that he intended to break away from lightly. Not that Rachel had any wish for him to do that as she felt her body urging for even more contact with his own. The future, she declared to herself, was surely something that they could now face together for this was really where she belonged.

Returning a few minutes later Eric Taylor beamed with pride although his associate seemed to be none too sure about the developing situation.

"I thought you said that lass of yours was supposed to be costing up some of the equipment for your office Eric?"

"Blow any equipment for I consider that this is far more important. Anyway as nice as it all is I doubt if I would have the room to house any of it!"

"Are you trying to say that you came here on a ruse?"

"Now what do you take me for John? Would I do anything like that? I suggest we go and find ourselves a spot of lunch and leave the two of them to it. Somehow I don't think that girl will be coming back to Manchester with me tonight, which means I can make an early start back. That is something that will please the wife because she had invited visitors around tonight and if I am not present there will be hell to play! And as far as that lad over there is concerned, well I guess I always said that I would have to find him a wife!"

★ ★ ★ ★

Other Novels By Kathleen Steele

MARINA BAIXA - Romance and Intrigue leads from the security of the Lake District to uncertainty in Spain!

ARMS OF GOLD - Following September 11th, what connection does the Lakeat Windermere have with the Mediterranean around Majorca?

RADIANT VIBES - Pollution in the Irish Sea leads to strange findings and unusual relationships!

OASIS IN TIME - The location of those illusive weapons of mass destruction provides surprises!

PUT AND TAKE - Casinos on the Fylde Coast? Would you like to take a chance?

THE UPPER CUT - Scurrilous behaviour on those Upper Reaches serves to create ripples that stir those once still waters!

THE PINK ROSE - The Border Folk's response to the proposed Regional Assemblies brings mayhem!

TWO FACED - Buying a computer should require a Government Health Warning!

ROUND AND ROUND - Wind and Tide can make uneasy bedfellows in the struggle to find a new Power Source!

NEXT STOP PARADISE – Love and intrigue are stimulated on life's merry-go-round!

CHECK OUT - The development of the provincial Airport, heralds the development in human relationships

HIDE AND SEEK - Hidden treasures require attention to detail, or else----!

LOST AND FOUND - Where there's a will, there's a way!

FOOTLOOSE - When a positive charge meets a positive charge, then ------!

IN THE SHADOW OF THE STORM - Do the fish always behave like that or is this the calm before the storm?

DISTRACTION - A hidden cell in the Lake District leads to a tempest of ferocity which contrasts sharply with the peace and tranquillity that place is noted for!

A LIGHTER SHADE OF PINK - A sequel as requested to THE PINK ROSE. Meet the various characters again as this time our friends attempt to extend their franchise into Cumbria!

THE HEART'S REFRAIN - The mists around those magical Islands reflect the mist that obscures Anton's vision.

THE TURN OF THE WHEEL - Romance and fortune can be linked!

VENGEFUL RETURN - Two men and yet there can only ever be one boat! A sequel to MARINA BAIXA and NEXTSTOP PARADISE

NOT HERE - What is the connection between that house fire and those windmills out at sea?

THE RUN OF THE RABBIT - Could the government really be conspiring to move that Nuclear Power Plant into the midst of the Langdale Valley?

STAR OF THE DAWN - Can the star of early morning point the way to life's fulfilment?

SKETCH ME LOVE - The shrouding mist of those tranquil Islands serves to disguise a more sinister scheme to involve them in man's game!

SPLIT WIDE OPEN - Mischievous Pranks or mysterious happenings disturb the peace in the hamlet of FellBeck!

POWERFUL CIRCLES - What is the connection between those ancient customs and the future?

BISPHAM BROOK - Could this be the case where such water comes to create mayhem or is there something more sinister behind the apparently innocent flow?

CRAB ISLAND - The Atlantic Isles offer peace, tranquillity and dramatic scenery to the innocent holidaymaker yet one cannot but speculate that there is something more!

SHAP - The fells of North West England may provide a refuge but other things also transpire in a community that proves that they are not quite so isolated!

INNER TURMOIL - Recovering from a trauma in her life Krisha is soon to find that the past often has a habit of catching up on one!

CRISP LIES THE TRACK - Will the ashes of the past support the love of today?

THE VIPER'S BITE - Beware of reptiles with warm blood in their veins!

SOFTLY THE NIGHT - Rags to riches perhaps?

VEIL OF SECRETS - Can love survive the tide of deception?

WEB OF TORMENT - When the storm infiltrates, can peace survive?

STRICTURES OF THE HEART - Eruption serves to spark the heart.

ECHOES FROM THE PAST - Harmony sounds a discordant note.

A NATURAL CHOICE - Water water everywhere, be careful where you step.

AN UNEVEN STEP - Can the murderer be found in the most unlikely of circumstances?

THE CURTAIN RISES - When evil strikes, can love prevail?

TIME STOOD STILL - Will time reveal its hidden secrets?

HIGHWAY TO LOVE - Can fortune's treasures find true love?

HEADING INTO INTRIGUE - When the door closes can love survive?

If you have difficulty in obtaining any of the above copies contact 01253 591905

PASSPORT

with feeling

Words an
Jin

Tempo: 90

Page 1